Julia

Melinda Metz

HarperTrophy®

A Division of HarperCollinsPublishers

Produced by 17th Street Productions, Inc.
33 West 17th Street, New York, NY 10011

Library of Congress Catalog Card Number: 99-066678
ISBN 0-06-440814-0

For my parents

Hear ye, hear ye,
all noble folk of the land of Manhattan:

Donald W. Reed, King of Medicine, and
Amelia L. Prescott, Queen of Finance, wish to
announce the birth of their princess,

Julia Anastasia Reed-Prescott.

Princess Julia arrived late on the night of
March 3, announcing her presence with a
royal wail that seemed much too loud
to have emerged from her delicate
5-pound, 11-ounce, $18\frac{1}{2}$-inch body.

The princess will be delighted to meet her
subjects on the afternoon of March 8,
between the hours of 1 and 4, at the castle,
300 Central Park West,
The Penthouse.

MEET MY BABY GIRL /
CELEBRATE THE REMOVAL
OF MY BALL AND CHAIN /
GARAGE SALE

(size 7 clothes, size 8 shoes, assorted perfume, makeup, bath oil, etc.) PARTY

March 8
8 to WHENEVER
1173 Ridge Highway, Brooklyn

BYOB and a baby present for Maggie. Anyone who mentions the name Annette gets booted. No exceptions.

Luke Watkins
Maggie's stats—Born 3/3,
5 pounds, 11 ounces, 18 1/2 inches.
And growing like crazy.

To Do List for Julia's First Birthday Party

- Rent Central Park castle and carousel.

- Order cake from Colette (mention that you loved what she did for White House Christmas)—castle with working drawbridge and flowing hot fudge moat.

- Order invitations—parchment paper scrolls with silk ribbons.

- Hire actor (Lincoln Square theater?) to hand-deliver invitations dressed in suit of armor (borrow from Met?).

- Have Julia fitted for authentic medieval princess outfit.

- Gift baskets for parents from Godiva.

- Prizes for kids from FAO Schwarz.

- Arrange for pony rides—ponies to have garlands on reins, braided manes and tails, etc.

- Invite *Times* society editor—the new one.

- Hire band of strolling musicians (Juilliard students?).

- Ask Luciano if he'll sing "Happy Birthday."

- Instruct juggler to give lessons to anyone who fancies.

- Have announcement made before joust that it's just play so children won't be frightened.

- Instruct puppeteer that show should have Julia and Tyler as the names of the princess and prince.

- Tactfully ask the mayor not to solicit contributions from the guests.

Stuff to do for Maggie's b·day party.

- Order ice·cream cake from Carvel.

- Get 2x chips, dip, and drinks as last time.

- Buy extra wipes.

- Clean john!

- Ask Lynette if she'll come over early
  and help decorate. No balloons. Kids
  can choke on balloons.

What should I name my new pony?

Abercrombe
Flan
Madonna
Madison
Perrier
Tutu
Huxtable
Bubbles
Madeline
Whitney
Beemer
Taffeta

What I could name the gerbil Dad gave me for my sixth birthday

Gap

Pudding

Madonna

Atlantic

Pepsi

Sneaker

Huxtable

Caffeine

Madeline

Whitney

Bug

Denim

Dear Diary,

   You're the best present I got on my birthday. (Even though my mother didn't think you were nice enough because you're a present from Sarah. And the present I got Sarah for her birthday cost a lot more. Stuff like that is important to my mother. She says it's about good manners. It seems like it's just about $$$.)

   Now that I'm twelve, I know I'm going to have a ton of secret stuff to tell you. Stuff I won't be able to tell anyone else. Because twelve is just a lot different than eleven. Twelve is really the same as being a teenager. Almost.

   I don't have any good gossip or anything yet. But I'm sure starting tomorrow—my first full day as a twelve-year-old—I'll have all kinds of exciting things to tell you.

   Bye for now.

                              Love,
                              Julia Reed-Prescott

P.S. What do you think of the name Julia? I think it sounds like an old lady name. Maybe from now on I'll tell people to call me Jules. Or JuJu—like that candy. Sigh. Like my mother would ever let me have a cool nickname like that.

Hi, Diary,

I feel kind of stupid writing to you like you were a person or something. Maybe I'll get used to it. I just got you today for my twelfth birthday. I think I'll give you a name so I won't feel so dorky. How about JuJu—after my favorite candy JuJu Bees?

Okay. Dear JuJu. I think I'll be talking to you a lot. Now that I'm twelve, there's going to be tons of stuff I can't talk to Dad about. Like getting my period. Can you imagine the look on his face if I tried to talk to him about that—when it happens? He'd try to keep his face all normal, but he wouldn't be able to really look at me. And since Mom went out for cigarettes three days after I was born and never came back—at least that's the way Dad tells it—I'll have to talk to you.

But tomorrow, okay? 'Cause I'm too sleepy to write.

Good night.

Love ya,
Maggie

Mrs. Channing Keyes
Principal, the Warriner School
1530 Riverside Drive
New York, New York

Dear Mrs. Keyes,

It is my pleasure to write a letter of recommendation for Julia Reed-Prescott. Julia has been a student at the Bradford Academy since the first grade. She has proven herself to be a hardworking, diligent student with a fine mind. On a personal note, Julia has impeccable manners and can always be counted on to set a good example for her classmates. I cannot think of a student who would be a better asset to your school than Julia.

Enclosed are a copy of Julia's transcripts. Please feel free to call me if you would like to discuss Julia's qualifications in more depth, or sit next to me at the literacy tea and I can fill you in there. Julia's mother will be in attendance as well. I'm sure you know her or at least know of her—Amelia Prescott. She has always been most generous in her contributions to our school, and I know Warriner is her first choice for Julia to get the preparation she needs to attend the college of her choice.

See you at the tea.

With warmest best wishes,

Snookie

Miss Suzanne Martel
Headmistress
The Bradford Academy

Mr. Luke Watkins
1173 Ridge Highway
Brooklyn, NY

Dear Mr. Watkins,

I would like you to make an appointment with me at your earliest convenience to discuss Maggie's performance at school. Maggie is a bright girl, with real potential. I can easily see her getting a college scholarship in a few years.

But only if she applies herself. The number of classes Maggie has missed this semester is alarming, as is the number of homework assignments she has failed to turn in. I would like the two of us to set up a system to more closely monitor Maggie's progress. Next year she'll be moving on to an even bigger school, where I'm afraid it will be very easy for her to fall through the cracks. Let's make sure that doesn't happen.

Sincerely,

Tess Cookson

Tess Cookson
Guidance Counselor
PS 107

<u>Letter</u> to <u>myself</u>
<u>on</u> <u>my</u> <u>fifteenth</u> birthday

I read an article in a magazine that said you should write yourself a letter on every birthday. I decided to do it, starting now.

When I think about my year as a fourteen-year-old, I see lots of areas where I could have done better. Here is a list.

1. French grade—not acceptable if I want to get into a first-rate college.
2. Extracurricular activities. Only holding one office—especially when that office is treasurer, the pity office—is not acceptable, ditto, ditto.
3. I think Tyler might want to break up with me. And my mother says Tyler and I are perfectly matched. So I think I should get extensions. Mom thinks if I do, I'll look just like Brandy. Tyler thinks Brandy is hot.
4. I need to speak up more when Mom and Dad introduce me to their friends. I should come up with a list of charming, amusing, appropriate anec-dotes to use when necessary. Plus I have to

remember to smile more but not so much that I look like an imbecile. No more invisible girl.

5. Find a way to improve myself every day. Even if it's just learning a new vocabulary word.

I think if I follow this list carefully that when I write myself my letter on the event of my next birthday—which is going to be so amazing because my mom's already started planning my Sweet Sixteen party—my life will be much, much better.

Sincerely,
Julia Reed-Prescott

Dear Me,

  Okay, this mag said to write a letter to yourself on your birthday. I thought it would be cool
to do it so I'd have them to read when I get old.
(Hi, old me!) Maybe even give them to my daughter to read someday. If I ever have a daughter.
Which probably I won't. Because I really don't
see myself getting married. Ever. And the single-
parent thing? I don't think it's fair to the kid.
Why make them start out life with one strike
against them?

  So anyway. Today is my fifteenth birthday.
My year as a fourteen-year-old was . . . decent.
I'm not going to lie. It wasn't great. It wasn't some
kind of glory days, like in that old song my dad
always listens to. But I had/have some friends I
like to hang with. We're not popular. We're not
unpopular. We're sort of in that invisible space
between popularity and that group for whom
school is one endless ball of pain.

  My dad and I got along fairly decently.
Although he still doesn't realize that I'm pretty
much an adult. I mean, hello, he got my mom
pregnant when he was about a year older than I
am now, and he started taking care of me on his

own, like, nine months and three days later. So, really, I'm way old enough to decide what time I can come home and all that.

On the boyfriend front—big nada. Could it be because I have no visible breasts? Are guys that shallow? That would be yes! Which is fine by me. A lot of my friends are getting all gaga over some guy. It kind of makes me sick. And the idea of having some guy stick his tongue down my throat—can I say yuck?

And that about wraps it up. So bye old me until my next birthday. That one's going to be a killer, probably my very best ever—my Sweet Sixteen.

Love and kisses,
Maggie

Julia Reed-Prescott met the eyes of her driver in the rearview mirror and gave him a polite smile. It was the appropriate smile for the circumstances—not so friendly that the driver would assume that she wanted him to start a conversation with her, but not so unfriendly that the driver would get the impression that Julia thought she was somehow better than he was just because he was getting paid to drive her to Brooklyn.

chapter

1

She wished that her mother's company used limos instead of sedans for their business cars, limos with tinted, soundproof glass between the driver and the passenger. That way Julia wouldn't have to try to keep her expression pleasant. That way she could bury her head in her hands and cry, cry, cry until her body was completely dehydrated and it was impossible to squeeze out even one more tear.

But that wouldn't be appropriate in a sedan. Not in clear view of the driver. *His name is Alex,* she reminded herself. It was important to remember names.

Her mother always became so exasperated with Julia when she zoned out during introductions.

Julia turned and pressed her forehead against the window as they started across the Brooklyn Bridge. Her eyes began to sting, and she stared hard at the murky water of the East River. *Don't cry,* she ordered herself. *Don't even think about crying.*

Her cell phone rang, and she dug it out of her suede bag, happy for the distraction.

"Julia, it's me," Sydney Jane burst out before Julia even had a chance to say hello. Not good phone manners. "I have a Sweet-Sixteen-related news flash for you, and you're *not* going to like it."

"Go ahead," Julia said, struggling to keep her voice neutral.

"Okay, well, Tyler is coming to your party," Sydney Jane continued. Julia's supposed best friend sounded way too gleeful to be giving such hideous info.

"I knew that already," Julia told her, unable to prevent a tinge of annoyance from creeping into her tone. She'd been trying so hard not to cry—and now Sydney Jane was bringing up what Julia had been trying so hard not to cry *about.* What was Sydney Jane thinking? It wasn't as if Julia could forget that her ex-boyfriend, so newly ex that she still felt like there was a Tyler-Sanderson-shaped hole in her heart, was going to ruin what was supposed to be the best day in her life so far.

"I know," Sydney Jane rushed on. "But that's not all. Guess who he's bringing? No, you'll never guess. Let me tell you. He's bringing Elena Stratford."

Julia felt as if she'd been punched in the stomach. Not that she'd ever actually *been* punched in the stomach, but she was sure this was how it had to feel—pain so powerful, it made her dizzy.

"Did you hear me?" Sydney Jane demanded, sounding disappointed that Julia hadn't started screaming like a deranged maniac or something. Sydney Jane loved drama.

"Yes. Okay? Yes, I heard you," Julia snapped. She shot a guilty glance at the driver. She knew it wasn't appropriate to have any kind of squabble in front of a stranger. Even at home, behind closed doors, disputes were supposed to be dealt with in low, calm voices. "Can I call you back later?" Julia asked, her voice under control once more. "I'm about to go take the test to get my driver's permit."

"Did you hear me?" Sydney Jane asked again. "I said Elena Stratford and Tyler—"

Julia did something she'd never done in her whole life—not even to an irritating telemarketer. She hung up on someone. On a friend. She leaned her head back on the soft, nubby upholstery and squeezed her eyes shut.

Immediately a dozen little Elenas began dancing across the backs of her eyelids. Elenas with perfectly straight, supershiny dark brown hair and exotic almond-shaped eyes and full breasts.

Julia jerked open her eyes, but the Elenas didn't disappear. They multiplied until there were hundreds of tiny Elenas dancing all over the back of the sedan, that sexy kind of dancing Julia had never managed to figure out how to do, that kind of dancing where your body seemed to be liquid music, no inhibitions, no self-consciousness, just movement.

Don't even go there, she told herself. But it was too late. Hundreds of little Tylers had joined the Elenas, slow dancing, sliding their bodies together. The Tylers were smiling at the Elenas in a way that the real Tyler had never, ever smiled at Julia.

Julia's cell phone rang again, and the Tylers and Elenas blurred, then quickly disappeared. Julia grabbed the phone. "I'm really sorry, Syd, I—," she began.

"Is that any kind of way to answer a telephone?" Julia's mother interrupted.

"Oh, Mom." Julia cracked the window. She was starting to feel a little carsick. "I'm sorry. I wasn't thinking. I guess I'm just . . . nervous about the test to get my permit."

Which was probably the two-millionth lie she'd told her mother this year. Julia had studied for the test. The test was no problem. But seeing Tyler and Elena together at the party—Julia wasn't sure she'd survive it.

". . . aren't you, Julia?"

Julia's mother had just asked a question, and Julia had no idea what that question was. She'd spaced out. And that was one of the things her mother hated most. It was incredibly rude not to give the person you were conversing with your full and complete attention.

"Y-yes, I'm going straight to the Castle Spa when I leave the DMV," Julia said, taking a chance.

There was a pause, a long pause that felt worse than if her mother had started yelling at her.

"I asked why you couldn't have postponed the test until another day," her mother finally replied.

"My driving course starts on Monday," Julia reminded her mom. "I have to have a learner's permit by then, and I couldn't take the test before today because you have to be sixteen."

"And why Brooklyn?" her mother asked.

Julia muffled a sigh. For all that her mother went on

and on about how rude it was not to pay full and complete attention while conversing, she never seemed to hear anything Julia said.

"The teacher said that we should do all our driving tests in Brooklyn," Julia explained, just the way she'd explained that morning at breakfast.

Julia's mother hated Brooklyn. But Julia really liked it. It felt more neighborhoody. The buildings were shorter, and you could see more of the sky. Somehow it was easier to imagine real people living their lives here than in the huge, nosebleed-high building in which Julia and her parents lived.

Just watching the squat, homey buildings go by outside the window made her relax a little, even with her mother rattling off a list of key tasks that needed to be completed before the party, soon to become the worst experience of Julia's life.

"Tonight's going to be wonderful," Julia's mother said, wrapping up her list. "You're excited, aren't you?"

"Of course," Julia answered automatically.

The two-hundred-million-and-first lie. Why couldn't she ever say what she was really thinking?

"Actually, no. I'm not looking forward to it at all," Julia blurted out, surprising herself. "Mom, Tyler's bringing a date. I can't be there and see it. I can't. I'll go crazy. Couldn't I just call him up and politely, I don't know, uninvite him?"

Her mother sighed. "Julia, we've talked about this," she answered. "My company is in the middle of a merger with Tyler's father's. It's a very delicate situation. Besides, there is no such thing as uninvite. It isn't even a proper word."

Julia felt like letting out a shriek that would shatter every window in the car and all the traffic lights for blocks. This was her one and only Sweet Sixteen, and her mother cared more about some business deal, probably one of hundreds of business deals her mother had in the works.

But Julia didn't shriek. She didn't even raise her voice. Instead she pulled in a shaky breath, then quietly told her mother what she wanted to hear. "You're right. Uninvite is not a word, so how could I possibly uninvite Tyler?" she said. "We're almost to the DMV. I'll see you at home," she added.

"Don't worry about Tyler," her mother told her. "He's just being a boy. When he sees you in your Vera Wang, he's going to be begging for your forgiveness on his knees. You two belong together—we've all known that since you were babies. He'll remember that soon enough."

Julia gave a strangled sound that she hoped would pass for agreement. Then she waited for her mother to say good-bye and clicked off the phone.

"Here we go," the driver—Alex, Alex, Alex!—said as he pulled into the crowded DMV lot and swung the sedan into a slot with one smooth motion.

"Thanks, Alex," Julia answered. "I hope I won't keep you waiting too long. I don't know how the lines are going to be in there."

"Don't worry about it." He held up a copy of the new Grisham thriller and smiled.

Julia smiled back and climbed out of the car. *You're about to go through an important sixteenth-birthday ritual,* she told herself. *Just forget about Tyler and E—and everything else—until after the test.*

She smoothed her suede skirt, pulled a loose thread off the cuff of her cashmere coat, and headed through the dingy glass doors.

Her eyes immediately flew to a tall, broad-shouldered boy. He turned slightly, and the glow from his warm brown eyes lit up his perfect face. Those eyes! Those cheekbones! Those lips! Those lips! Those lips! An angel choir began to sing.

You absolutely must stop being so obsessive, Julia ordered herself. There were no little Tylers and Elenas in the car, and Tyler was *not* standing over there in his own personal spotlight.

Julia shook her head and gave three quick blinks. The angel choir stopped in mid-aaaah. The glow around Tyler disappeared.

But Tyler remained.

It's fate, a breathy little voice exclaimed in Julia's head.

No, she told herself. *It's the fact that Tyler is signed up for classes at the same driving school as you are, which has a lot to do with your mother and his father and nothing to do with fate,* she continued her internal lecture. *Look, Daniel Choate is here too. And why? Because he's in the same class and he has to get his permit before Monday too and this is where the teacher said to come. Again, nothing to do with fate. Or destiny. Or karma. Or anything romantic like that.*

Julia knew that all this was true, but she couldn't stop herself from taking a step toward Tyler. *It's fate,* the breathy little voice insisted again.

Maybe the little voice was right. Maybe it was fate that she and Tyler belonged together. Julia took another step toward him.

Everyone who knows us thinks we're a perfect couple, she thought. *It's fate,* the breathy voice jumped in again. Julia took another step toward Tyler. Then another.

9

One more step and he would see her. One more step and he would take her in his arms and beg her forgiveness. One more step and he—

"I heard you bagged Elena for the party tonight. Way to go," Daniel said, loud enough for Julia and half the people in the DMV to hear.

"What I'm looking forward to is what happens *after* the party," Tyler answered. And he gave a low laugh.

The tears Julia had been trying so hard to keep inside began to spill down her cheeks, so hot, they felt like they were leaving burn marks on her skin.

She glanced wildly around the big room. She couldn't cry here. Not in front of everyone. It would be so embarrassing, so rude.

Julia spotted the ladies' room and bolted.

MONDAY
    Give Tyler a big 💋
    Study for French test

TUESDAY
    Tell Tyler I 💙 him
    Study for French test

WEDNESDAY
    French test
    4:00 flute lesson
    Outline Chaucer essay

THURSDAY
    Lunch Meet with Helping Hands committee re fund-raiser
    6:00 Meet Dad at Met—unless he cancels again
    Start Chaucer essay
    Review chapter 4 for history exam

FRIDAY
    Finish Christmas shopping
    Do trig practice test

SATURDAY
    8:00 Driving test
    10:00 Castle Spa
    8:00 Party

SUNDAY
    Call Grandma R.
    Start thank-you notes for b-day presents
    Remember Mom's charity auction committee is meeting at house
    Work on Chaucer essay

Maggie Watkins met her father's eyes in the rearview mirror for only a fraction of a second before he flicked them away. She frowned at him.

"What?" he asked, shooting another rapid glance at her before returning his attention to the road.

"You tell me," Maggie answered. She always knew when her father was hiding something. And he was hiding something big. She'd suspected it for two days, and now she was sure of it. It wasn't a good something, either, like some amazing present for her Sweet Sixteen. Those brackets on the sides of his mouth didn't deepen for good somethings.

chapter 2

If her dad had been hiding a good something, Maggie would have waited and let him surprise her. But if there was something bad headed her way, she wanted to know about it so she could start figuring out how to deal. Best defense was a good offense. She totally believed that.

Maggie's father leaned forward, staring at the road

intently, as if it were a minefield. "Uh, I probably should have told you this before, baby," he said. "But your . . . your . . . well, you see, I know it's going to come as a shock so I—"

"What?" Maggie exploded. "What?"

Her father almost never beat around the bush, and it was starting to make her nervous.

He cleared his throat. "You're . . . uh . . . mother is coming to the party tonight," he finished quietly.

Maggie stared at him in disbelief. Her mind galloped and her mouth moved before any sounds came out. "No way! Absolutely no way!"

"I don't like it, either," her dad answered. "But she *is* your mother."

"No, she's not! *You're* my mother!" Maggie shouted. All the blood seemed to rush from her head, making her feel dizzy and disoriented. "Or maybe I'm my own mother. But whatever, Annette *definitely* is not my mother. You don't get to be a mother if you've seen your kid three days in her whole entire life."

"Please, Maggie. She wants to see you now. She came all the way from California, and I—" her father began.

Maggie shot a look in the right lane. It was clear.

She leaned over, grabbed the wheel, and jerked the car into a screeching turn. "Take me to the bus stop!" she cried. "If Annette's coming to my party, I'm not even going to be in the same state."

"Maggie! What are you doing?" her father yelled. He pulled over to the curb and stopped so fast that Maggie had to brace her hands on the dashboard. "That was stupid! You could have killed us both."

"Right now, I think I'd rather be dead!" Maggie yelled back. She unbuckled her seat belt and jumped out of the car. Her father was out a second later. He strode around to face her, and they squared off, locking eyeballs.

How long is he going to hold out? Maggie wondered, staring into her father's hard, dark brown eyes.

Doesn't matter, she told herself. *However long it is, I'm holding out longer.* Maggie opened her eyes a little wider, ignoring the way they were starting to sting and burn. She used every bit of her will to keep them nailed on her father.

Her father ran his fingers over his face and up across his shaved head. "She didn't just leave you, you know. She left me, too," he finally said, so softly, Maggie almost didn't hear him.

With those words, all of Maggie's anger drained

away. Her dad hardly ever let her see his hurt. Sometimes he'd sit out in their tiny, all-cement back-yard, just staring off into space. She always thought he was thinking about her mother at those times, but he never said anything.

"So why let her come?" Maggie asked. She reached out and tugged the sleeve of her father's denim shirt.

He shrugged. "It seems like the right thing to do. Your Sweet Sixteen, it's a big deal. It's not like your wedding or anything. But it's still big. If she wants to be there . . ." He shrugged again.

"It's more than big; it's huge," Maggie agreed. "And she's going to ruin it for me." She hated the weak, whiny sound that had crept into her voice. But didn't her dad get how important her Sweet Sixteen was to her?

"Mags, what do you want me to do?" He ran his hands across his head again. "Maybe your . . . Annette could come by before the party. You two could see each other alone instead."

The thought of that was like a punch in the stomach. She still remembered how dizzy she'd gotten when Andy Miller had socked her one in the sixth grade. That was exactly how she felt now.

Maggie slid back into the car, her knees a little too Jell-O-like to stand, and shut the door with a soft click. A moment later her father climbed back behind the wheel. "Well?" he asked.

"At the party," Maggie muttered. She knew there was no way to get around seeing Annette. Her dad was obviously not going to bend on this one. And if Maggie had to do it, she wanted to be in a crowded place, where she could say two words to the woman and then hang with her friends the rest of the night.

Yeah, that sounded *real* fun. That sounded like the party she'd been dreaming about for *years*. But still, it was a lot better than actually having to survive a big heart-to-heart alone with some stranger. That would make her gag.

"Are you still up for taking the test?" her father asked. "Or you want to postpone?"

"I can handle it," Maggie answered.

He reached over and gave her earlobe a gentle tug. "You can handle anything," he said. He pulled a U and headed back in the direction of the DMV.

Maggie smiled at him. *I wonder if I look like her?* The thought slammed into her head as she gazed at her father's face. He and Maggie didn't look anything

17

alike. He was kind of short and square. She was tall and slender. He had caramel-colored skin. Hers was more like milk chocolate. He had eyes so dark, they were almost black. Hers were so light, they were almost golden.

She'd always wished she looked more like him. Although she had to admit that she was probably prettier than she would have been if she'd come out looking like a girl version of her father, all stubby and everything. It's just that families should look alike. And especially when she was a little girl, there was nothing Maggie had wanted more than for absolutely everyone to know with one glance that she and her dad were a family.

It would be so wrong if Maggie ended up looking like Annette. Maggie didn't want the slightest connection to link them. Not even the shape of their eyebrows.

"Here we go." Her father swung the car into the DMV parking lot and zipped into a place. "You sure you don't want me to wait and drive you to work?"

"Nah. There's a bus that goes from here to practically right in front of the Burger Castle," Maggie answered.

"Okay, see you when you get home. Good luck," he said.

Maggie got out of the car. *Okay, just forget about Ann—forget about everything until after the test. This is a big moment—the first step on your way to your license and freedom. Enjoy it.*

She hurried through the DMV's dingy glass doors. *Oh, great,* she thought as she scanned the crowd. *More than half these people don't even live in Brooklyn.*

She hated the way all the rich Manhattan kids used her borough as their driving kindergarten. They all took their tests and their classes over here. Probably so if they got in a fender bender they wouldn't wreck a limo or some vintage car or whatever people drove on the other side of the bridge.

A lot of Maggie's friends liked to spend as much time as possible in The City (always pronounced so you could hear the capital *T* and *C*). But Maggie hated it. All that gourmet coffee and those expensive clothes and plastic-looking faces. Disgusting. There were even parts of Brooklyn she avoided because they felt too much like Manhattan.

Maggie got in line behind a twinset-wearing, *Vogue*-reading, reeking-of-vanilla-cappuccino girl with those stupid little minibuns all over her empty head.

"I don't know you, but I hate you already," she muttered.

The girl looked over her shoulder. "What?" she demanded in her snotty, silky voice.

"Nothing," Maggie answered. She imagined herself reaching over and ripping one of the girl's minibuns right off.

"No, tell me what you said." The girl spun around—and sent a shower of her vanilla cappuccino across Maggie's only winter coat.

"I said, why don't you go back where you belong?" Maggie yelled. Without waiting for an answer, she strode toward the ladies' room, hoping she could salvage her coat. She didn't want to walk around with a big, stinky stain for the rest of the winter.

The second she opened the bathroom door, she heard the sound of crying from one of the stalls. Perfect. Just what she needed.

Maggie ignored the weeper—probably some loser rich kid who flunked the test—and headed for the sink. She grabbed a sheet of the rough brown paper toweling and ran it under the cold water. The crying got louder.

Oh, please. Maggie gave an exaggerated sigh. "Do

you need a tissue or something?" she snapped. She wasn't really enjoying listening to this girl snivel.

"I'm sorry," a watery voice answered. Then the door of the closest stall slowly swung open—

Maggie stared at the girl. She raised her hand to her forehead and, for the second time in an hour, she felt dizzy enough to faint.

MONDAY

Grocery shop—remember Dad's on Atkins diet

TUESDAY

Probably reading quiz—if Mr. L. sticks to pattern of "surprise" quizzes

WEDNESDAY

 4–9

Spanish test

 ## THURSDAY

Feed Mrs. T.'s

FRIDAY

Feed Mrs. T.'s
New Big Willie movie opens today

SATURDAY

Driver's test

 10–3

Scoz
PARTY!!!

SUNDAY

Recover from PARTY!!

"Oh my God."

"W-wait. What?" Julia stammered. She stepped through the stall door, locked eyes with the girl standing by the sink, and then froze.

Julia couldn't take her eyes off the girl. Neither of them moved or said anything more for at least a minute. Julia pressed her fingertips against her lips, trying to collect some words. "Um, am I having a break with reality, or do you look exactly like me?"

The girl shook her head abruptly as if to clear it. After another moment of shocked silence she snapped, "Make that *you* look like *me*. And not exactly. I don't have any desire to look like a Brandy clone."

Julia ran her hair through her long, cascading curls and took a nervous peek in the mirror. A rush of heat flooded her face.

"So, who are you, anyway?" the girl asked. She sounded flippant, but her eyes were intent on Julia's face.

"I'm Julia Reed-Prescott," Julia replied. She stuck out her hand. "And you are?"

chapter

3

The girl just stared at her appraisingly.

Julia's face grew even hotter. What was the problem? She was just trying to be polite, and this girl was acting as if Julia was some kind of sideshow attraction. Not that Julia had ever been to a sideshow attraction. But she had heard of them. And that's how she felt right now, like a person in a cage being stared at by a snickering, superior—

"My name's Maggie Watkins," the girl announced. She didn't offer to shake hands. "And it's not like I want to start having some kind of *Sister, Sister* moment with you or anything, but we do look exactly alike. This is crazy."

Julia started backing toward the door. She felt like this was a dream, and she had a sudden urge to wake up. Maggie Watkins really did look like she could be Julia's twin—looking at her was like looking in a mirror, except this girl wasn't looking friendly.

Maggie shook her head. "I thought all you rich girls were supposed to be so well-bred. I'm sure you go to one of those fancy prep schools. Didn't they even teach you to wash your hands before you leave the bathroom?"

"Of course," Julia answered. If her skin got any hotter, it would combust. A picture flashed through her mind—flames shooting out of her face, charring the sinks, boiling the water in the toilets, and setting Maggie's ultrashort hair on fire.

Maggie raised her eyebrows and gave a pointed look at the sink behind her.

"But I didn't . . . I didn't . . ." What word was Julia supposed to use here?

Maggie snorted. "Oh, I forgot. Brandy dolls aren't anatomically correct. You don't need to go."

"Why are you being so mean to me?" Julia burst out. She couldn't believe she'd spoken the words aloud.

Maggie was quiet for a minute. Then she sighed. "I'm sorry," she finally said.

And weirdly, she actually did sound sorry. Not sarcastic. Not mocking.

"I've just had the most hideous day," Maggie continued. She glanced at her watch. "And it's only twenty after eight." She half sat on the edge of the nearest sink as if she was too tired to stand up anymore.

"Tell me about it." Julia walked over to the sink next to Maggie's. She thought about sitting on it, but it was way too easy for her to imagine herself sliding right off, so she just leaned.

Maggie reached behind her and tore off a fresh sheet of paper towel. She handed it to Julia. "You might want

25

to blow your nose," she suggested, but in a friendly way.

Julia blew, then crumpled the paper towel and tossed it in the trash. "I've never done that in front of anyone before," she admitted. "My mother thinks it's disgusting to blow your nose in public." A smile tugged at her lips. "Sometimes I think *she's* not anatomically correct."

The burst of laughter from Maggie surprised Julia. But the sound of Maggie's ridiculously high giggles made her crack up, too. She laughed hard, hard enough to bring new tears to her eyes, hard enough to make her let out a machine-gun explosion of snorts.

"I bet . . . I bet you never did *that* before, either," Maggie choked out between giggles. She pointed at Julia. "The piglet from Manhattan!" she exclaimed, then she started snorting twice as loudly as Julia had, which Julia wouldn't have thought possible.

"Stop . . . please stop," Julia cried. She pressed her hands over her stomach. "You're . . . hurting me!" She didn't think she'd ever laughed like this before, with her mouth stretched open wide and the rest of her face all squinched up and loud, loud, loud. Her mother always told Julia her laugh tended to get horsey and unattractive if she wasn't careful, so Julia usually tried to stick to smiling.

"I can't stop," Maggie answered, her words coming

out breathless. She started to rock back and forth, uttering sounds that were more like howls than laughter.

Julia leaned back her head, wiped her eyes with the back of one hand, and managed to get control of herself. "I can't even remember what we were laughing about."

"Me neither," Maggie admitted. She gave a couple of last snorts, then silence filled the bathroom.

"So this is—," Julia began.

"Pretty freaky," Maggie finished. She stood up and turned to face the long mirror over the sinks. Julia turned around, too.

They really were identical, except for superficial things, like clothes, and hairstyle, and makeup. Of course, Julia's eyes were redder and puffier from crying. And Maggie wore a knowing smirk unlike any expression Julia had ever tried on.

I wonder what my life would be like if I was her? Julia thought suddenly.

"So what was wrong before?" Maggie asked, speaking to Julia's reflection.

"You go first," Julia answered. "Why was today so hideous?"

Maggie didn't turn to face Julia. She kept her focus on the image of Julia in the mirror.

"This woman, Annette . . . my . . . my mother, actually, is coming to my Sweet Sixteen party tonight," Maggie admitted.

"It's my Sweet Sixteen tonight, too!" Julia exclaimed.

"No way!" Maggie cried. "It really is like some bizarre separated-at-birth scenario. But that's totally impossible. I almost wish it wasn't." She shot a quick glance at the real Julia. "That way it would be *our* mother coming to *our* Sweet Sixteen. I wouldn't have to deal by my—" Maggie shook her head. "We should get back out there and take the test."

"No, tell me," Julia insisted. "I don't understand. Weren't you expecting your mother to come to your party?"

Maggie seemed to suddenly remember she had a wet paper towel in her hand. She started scrubbing at the front of her coat, not looking at Julia or Julia's reflection. "My . . . *Annette* took off three days after I was born. I've never even met her, never even *spoken* to her. And now she just announces to my dad that she's coming to my party." Her paper towel started to shred, but Maggie kept rubbing and rubbing.

Julia didn't know what to say. A lot of her friends had divorced parents. A friend from school's father had died the year before. But to know that your own mother had been out there in the world somewhere for sixteen years and didn't even care enough to make a phone call . . .

"And *I* was the one crying in the bathroom," Julia said softly. She reached over and pulled the mangled paper towel out of Maggie's fingers. "That's really awful about your mom."

Maggie grabbed another paper towel and wet it. Then threw it in the trash. "It's hopeless," she said. She was staring at the stain on her coat, but Julia was pretty sure that wasn't what Maggie was talking about.

"You should go to *my* party," Julia said. "All I have to complain about is an ex-boyfriend who's coming with Elena Stratford, the most beautiful girl in school and possibly the universe. Much more beautiful than me," she finished quietly.

"You're letting your ex-boyfriend come to your party? Are you insane?" Maggie exclaimed. "Kick the guy to the curb. And by the way, I hope I didn't just hear you call me a dog. Because if you think you're a dog compared to this Elena chick, then I have to be a dog, too."

"You're not a dog," Julia said quickly. Maggie, standing over there in her tight jeans, battered pink boots, and T-shirt with *attitude* spelled out in rhinestones, was the kind of girl Tyler would call hot.

But if Maggie could be hot, then didn't Julia have to have the potential to be hot, too? Although not in a below-the-knee suede skirt and oatmeal-colored turtleneck. Turtlenecks were by definition not hot, weren't they? Maybe if she didn't wear turtlenecks so much, Tyler—

"You can call him up from here," Maggie continued. She jerked her chin toward the pay phone next to the tampon machine. "Just uninvite him."

"The thing with Tyler—," Julia began to explain.

"Tyler? The scum's name is Tyler?" Maggie interrupted. "I can't believe you're all upset over a guy named Tyler. I haven't even seen him, and I already know you can do better."

"The thing is, he's the son of the man who owns the company my mother's company is merging with. And his family and my family have been friends since before Tyler and I were born," Julia explained. "So I can't kick him to the curb." She'd never heard that expression before, but she loved it.

"Oh, man. I wish I could go to your party for you. I would have no problem making *Tyler* very sorry he even thought about showing up."

Julia smiled, but only for an instant. "After that, could you make him fall back in love with me?" she asked.

30

"You're pathetic," Maggie burst out. Then her expression softened. "When did you break up?" she asked.

Before Julia could answer, the ladies'-room door started to swing open. "Forget about it! Cleaning crew in here!" Maggie barked. The door slammed shut. "So when did you break up?"

Julia took Maggie's wrist and turned it until she could see Maggie's watch. "He kicked me to the curb two days, twenty-two hours, and eleven minutes ago. He said—he said—" Julia felt tears sting her eyes for about the millionth time since the breakup. "He said I was boring. He said I never wanted to do anything fun. He said—" She blinked rapidly to keep the tears from falling. "He said that every time he was with me, all he did was try to figure out the soonest he could take me home so he could go hang with his friends."

"You do *not* want this guy back," Maggie said firmly.

"I shouldn't even be talking about this to you," Julia answered. "The situation with your mother, that's so much worse. And here I am crying—"

"Please," Maggie interrupted. "Both our Sweet Sixteens are going to crash and burn. Maybe you and I should just go out tonight and celebrate our birthdays together."

"It would be fun," Julia answered. Maggie was so

different from any of the girls Julia knew. Spending time with her would be a complete adventure.

Maggie sighed. "Except my dad has been planning this party for weeks. If I didn't show . . . I couldn't do that to him."

"Maybe I should go to your party for you," Julia joked. "You could deal with Tyler for me. And I could make polite chitchat with your mother. I'm excellent at making polite chitchat."

Maggie stared at Julia's reflection for a long moment. "You know what? We should do it!" Maggie exclaimed, her eyes glittering with a dangerous excitement.

"We can't," Julia protested. "I mean, not really." She took a step away from Maggie.

"Of course we can!" Maggie insisted. "We trade clothes. We cut your hair. Do you have any scissors?"

"We can't," Julia repeated again. *Although it would be so wonderful to slip into someone else's life for one night, where there was no Tyler and no Elena and no merger . . .*

"Of course we can," Maggie repeated. She pulled Julia's suede bag off her shoulder and started digging through. "A platinum card. Whoa," she muttered. She kept digging. "I guess these won't really do it, huh?" Maggie held up a pair of nail scissors.

"I have an appointment at the Castle Spa right after

I leave here," Julia told her. "They sell wigs." She didn't know why she'd volunteered that. She shouldn't be encouraging Maggie.

"Perfect. I'll go to the appointment and use your card to buy myself a wig." She snapped her fingers. "You can tell my dad that your shift at work today was just a setup, that your Burger Castle friends chipped in and sent you to Just Hair for extensions as a birthday surprise. Come on. Let's trade clothes." Maggie pulled off her coat—denim lined with fake fleece. "Sorry about the stain."

Julia unfastened the top button on her cashmere coat. "Are we really going to do this?" she asked. Her heart started pounding. "We can't really do this." She undid another button. "We don't know each other well enough to pull it off." She unfastened the last two buttons.

"I give you complete and total authority to snoop through my stuff for info," Maggie said. "Plus even if we act weird, no one will guess the truth. What, they're going to go—'Hmmm, Julia's acting strange. She must have traded places with an identical stranger.'"

Julia giggled. "You're right," she answered. She was starting to feel excited in spite of herself. "You can read my diary or whatever you want. You could even go on-line and read my old e-mails." She slid off her coat and handed it to Maggie. "My password is—" She hesitated. "Don't laugh. My password is princess."

Maggie laughed. Julia laughed, too. "You have my cell phone in the purse. So I can call you if I need to," Julia said. "And if you can just jot down directions for where I'm supposed to go after we leave here . . ."

"So we're really doing this?" Maggie asked.

"You're the one who said we were," Julia answered. "Were you just kidding?" The heaviness of disappointment began to seep through her.

"No. It's totally insane, but I would do pretty much anything not to have to go to my own Sweet Sixteen," Maggie said.

"Me too." Julia rushed into the closest stall and unzipped her suede skirt. When she heard Maggie in the next stall, she tossed the skirt to her.

Five minutes later she stepped back out of the stall. She felt a little like a comic book hero who had just made the transformation into supergirl—not that Julia had been allowed to read comic books. Somehow she felt . . . stronger now that she was standing in Maggie's funky pink boots.

"I feel like . . . I don't even know what I feel like," Maggie said. She adjusted the neck of the sweater.

"You look amazing," Julia told her. How could Maggie wear the exact clothes she'd been wearing with so much style?

"So do you, JuJu," Maggie answered. She ran her hand back and forth over the sleeve of the cashmere coat as if she couldn't believe how soft it was.

"What did you just call me?" Julia cried.

Maggie turned and studied herself in the mirror. "JuJu. You know, like a nickname for Julia. Actually, it's what I call my diary."

"That's so crazy." Julia shook her head. "When I was twelve, I was dying to be called JuJu. But my mother had a fit—or her version of a fit, which is very quiet."

"Well, that's what I'm calling you from now on," Maggie said. She turned back to Julia. Her face was serious. "Good luck out there, JuJu."

"You too," Julia answered. "And have a wonderful Sweet Sixteen."

Mr. Donald W. Reed

and

Mrs. Amelia L. Prescott

request the pleasure of your company

at a party for their daughter,

Julia

to celebrate her sixteenth birthday

on

Saturday, December 22

8 o'clock

The Grand Ballroom

The Pierre Hotel

Fifth Avenue and 62nd Street

Black Tie

You're Invited!

TO: Maggie Watkins's Sweet Sixteen!

Where: Recreation Room at St. Regis Church

422 Seventh Avenue, Brooklyn

When: Saturday, December 22, 8:00 P.M.

Maggie's face grew drier and tighter as her facial mask hardened. It was her first mask ever. She was a soap-and-water girl. It worked for her—she didn't get many zits or stuff—so she figured why bother with anything else.

But lying back in a supercomfy reclining chair, with pads of something cool covering her eyes and soft music filling her ears, well, a girl could get used to this.

Maggie gave a start as a fingertip ran lightly down her cheek. "I'm sorry," the woman giving Maggie the facial said, her voice as gentle and soothing as the music. "Did you doze off? That happens a lot. I'm just going to rinse away the mask." The next thing Maggie felt was a warm cloth turning the mask back into silky-soft mud—or what felt like mud, anyway.

Enjoying the music and the chair and the feel of the mask on her skin was one thing. But having somebody wash her face for her—it just felt wrong. Not as wrong as having people wrap her in seaweed and

chapter

4

brush her skin with a loofah sponge—that had felt more than wrong. It had felt like she'd entered the twilight zone.

Maggie reached up and tried to take the cloth away from the woman. "I can just do it," she muttered.

"Relax," the woman answered, refusing to release her grip on the cloth. "I hear you have a big party coming up tonight. You're going to need all your energy for dancing."

Maggie took a deep breath and let it out slowly. But the muscles in her back and shoulders just got tighter. This was too freaky. Someone was getting paid to wash Maggie's face for her. Yeah, Maggie had a job in a "service industry." But she made burgers and fries. She didn't *feed* them to her customers and then wipe their mouths for them.

There wasn't enough money in the world for her to do something like that. Okay, maybe there was enough money in the *world*, but you had to add at least a zero to her Burger Castle wage.

"Are you sure you had a massage?" the woman said. She slid the pads off Maggie's eyes. "You're all knotted up."

Maggie cracked open her eyes and smiled at the woman. She looked like a nurse in her little white

40

smock. "I'm sure. I'm fine. Really," Maggie told her. The woman smiled back. She actually seemed to be enjoying her job. *I have to remember to give her a good tip,* Maggie thought, closing her eyes again.

Her muscles tightened up another notch. She had no idea what a good tip was in a place like this. She so did not belong here. Couldn't they tell that?

The woman wiped the last bit of mud from Maggie's face. A moment later she began rubbing in a thick, sweet-smelling cream, her fingers moving in a slow circular motion.

"You should really do this every night, especially in the winter," the woman told Maggie. "You have lovely skin, but there are traces of dryness in a few places."

Maggie snorted. A couple of jars of that cream would probably wipe out the little lump of cash she had stashed away to buy a computer.

"I'm sorry. Did I tickle your nose?" the woman asked.

"No, I almost sneezed, that's all," Maggie said quickly. Oh, man. She was doing stupid, unelegant—was that even a word?—stuff already. How was she going to get through the whole party without making a fool of herself?

Make that making a fool of Julia. Julia was the one

who would have to live with the mockery that would follow for weeks, possibly even years, if Maggie did something too public-school-Brooklyn-girl tonight.

A trill of electronic music interrupted Maggie's thoughts. Was it some kind of signal? Was someone supposed to rush in and clean the lint out of her belly button now? The same burst of music played again.

"Did you want to answer your cell?" the woman asked. "Or would you like me to turn it off for you?"

My cell, Maggie repeated silently. *Oh—my cell phone.* "I'll take it!" she exclaimed. A moment later the woman handed Maggie her purse. Maggie grabbed the phone, found the talk button, and said hello.

"Maggie, you've got to tell me what's on a Prince Burger," Julia blurted out in a rush. "I found a manual under one of the counters, but that page is ripped out."

"Lettuce, ketchup, grilled onions," Maggie answered automatically. "I'm glad you called. I need to ask you—"

"Uh, the manager is staring at me," Julia said, her voice almost inaudible.

Maggie's hand tightened on the little phone. "Please tell me you're not calling on Dan's office phone."

The only answer was the sound of the dial tone.

Great. Dan went nuts when employees used his phone. Maggie hoped she'd still have a job when Julia got through with her shift.

"Okay, we're done," the woman said. "I'll send in your manicurist now."

And she was gone before Maggie could even reach for her wallet. So did that mean that she wasn't supposed to tip? Maggie leaned forward and stared into the mirror in front of her. "Why don't you go back where you belong?" she whispered to herself.

Her eyes wandered down to the little table in front of the mirror. On it was a small, smoky green envelope with the name Denise written on it in perfect script.

Denise. Had the woman said her name was Denise when she first came into the room? Maggie couldn't remember. She'd been so caught up in taking in all the details of the beautiful little room—it was like the most luxurious dentist's office in the world, except without the scary instruments—that she'd totally spaced. But if Denise was the woman's name, then maybe the tip went in the envelope.

Maggie started to reach for it, then froze as the door slid open again and another woman in a white coat rolled in a little cart. Her jet black hair was pulled back in a bun so sleek, it looked almost like paint.

"Hello, I'm Josie," she said.

Josie, Josie, Josie, Maggie repeated to herself. If an envelope with the name Josie on it appeared next to the Denise one, Maggie was pretty sure she'd figured out the tip system.

"Let's start you off with a warm cream massage," Josie said. She took Maggie's left hand and squirted on a line of rich lotion a little warmer than Maggie's skin.

Maggie had to suppress a groan of pleasure as Josie began to work in the cream. Who knew that a hand could ever feel so good?

Her cell phone rang again. Maggie picked it up with her free hand. "I'm surprised you're not locked in the walk-in freezer," she said. "Did Dan totally bug out on you?"

One of Josie's eyebrows arched a little. Maggie felt heat work its way up her throat. Probably a girl like Julia, a girl who came to a place like this, wouldn't use an expression like that.

"Who is this?" a girl's voice asked. A girl's voice that wasn't Julia's. Oops.

"Who is *this?*" Maggie countered.

"It's Sydney Jane," the girl answered. "Julia, is that you?"

"Of course," Maggie answered, trying to modulate her voice to sound more like Julia's. "This is my cell phone; who else would it be?"

"What were you talking about—a what kind of freezer?" Sydney Jane asked. She didn't pause for an answer. "Never mind. I have more late-breaking news on the Tyler and Elena situation. Dorothea saw Elena at Saks, and Elena was trying on a dress that was cut so low in the back that you could almost see the top of her butt. And that's what she's wearing to your party!"

If this girl was a friend of Julia's, which it seemed as if she was, then she was sounding way too happy. If she was really talking to Julia right now, Julia would be crying again.

Lucky for Julia, Sydney Jane was on the phone with Maggie.

"That sounds pretty tacky, actually," Maggie answered.

There was a long pause on the other end of the phone. Josie finished the massage on her left hand, so Maggie switched the phone to it and gave Josie her right.

"Was there anything else you wanted to tell me?" Maggie said sweetly.

"I . . . I guess not," Sydney Jane replied. "You, um, sound a little weird."

"I have a cough," Maggie said, offering a brief cough as an example.

"Okay. Well, I'll see you at the party."

"See you there," Maggie answered. "Bye." She clicked off the phone.

She leaned back her head and closed her eyes, letting Josie work her magic. A girl really could get used to this.

"Did you bring a swatch from your dress so we could pick the right shade of polish?" Josie asked.

Maggie had managed—barely—to show up at enough home ec classes back in the eighth grade to know Josie wasn't asking for a plastic watch. "I think I remembered to put it in here," Maggie answered. She opened her purse and almost immediately found a square of shimmery material in a little plastic bag. It was white with just the faintest tinge of pink, so faint, it was hard to say for sure that it was really there.

"Beautiful," Josie whispered. "And I have just the thing." She held up a bottle of opalescent pale pink polish. It reminded Maggie of the inside of a seashell.

"Perfect," Maggie said.

After Josie had given Maggie's nails two coats of

46

polish, she started to work on Maggie's feet. She made them so soft and so smooth, Maggie wasn't sure she'd even be able to walk on them.

Perhaps Mummy and Daddy can hire someone to carry me about, she thought. She managed to stop herself from letting out another snort.

"All right. Now to the salon. Marcus has been working on the wig you picked out," Josie said. "Turn right and go in the last door at the end of the hall. He'll be expecting you." She gave Maggie one last smile and wheeled her cart out the door.

Maggie checked the little table and grinned. Another little envelope had magically appeared. *I'm getting the hang of this rich girl thing,* she thought. She opened her—well, Julia's—wallet. A neat row of twenties was lined up inside. She had to have at least three hundred bucks in there. Maggie never had that kind of cash on her—not even on grocery day.

Now all she had to do was figure out how much to leave in each envelope. When she and her dad went out to dinner, which they did every time she pulled in any A's on her report card, he doubled the tax because that was supposed to turn out to be the right percentage for the tip. But Maggie had no idea what the tax on a facial or a manicure was—because she had no clue what they cost.

I'll just give them both a twenty, she decided. Julia didn't have anything smaller than a twenty, anyway, and it wasn't as if there was a cashier Maggie could ask for change. She slipped a bill into each envelope and headed out into the hallway—almost running into a tall girl with dark brown hair and breasts like a centerfold.

"Oh, hello, Julia." The girl's eyes flicked to Maggie's short hair. "I didn't realize you wore extensions," she said. Her eyes traveled down to Maggie's hands. "Pink. That's so cute," she said. She had the same kind of voice as the gourmet-vanilla-cappuccino chick—snotty and silky at the same time. "I wish I could pull off the little-girl look. But"—she swept her hands down her body, showing off the curves—"on me it would look ridiculous. On you it's sweet. Really."

Would you still think it was sweet if my cute, little-girl pink nails were scratching your face? Maggie thought.

But she wasn't going to spoil her spa high by getting into a thing. "Whatever," she muttered. She turned and headed down to the salon. She reached for the door, then turned back. Yeah, the girl was staring after her. Maggie thought she'd felt eyes on her back.

Suddenly Maggie felt a rush of protectiveness for Julia. This cow clearly thought that she could stomp all over Julia with her big cow feet. She probably knew

Julia well enough to know she wouldn't fight back. How could she? Julia couldn't even blow her nose in public.

Maggie only had one day, but maybe she could change a few people's opinions about Julia and make them a little more careful about how they treated her.

"Oh, sweetie," Maggie called to the girl. "A word of advice. It would be a good idea to start wearing a bra with more support. I mean, the way you're built . . . well, I've seen women with boobs practically down to their knees. I would *hate* to see that happen to you."

Maggie didn't wait for a response. She turned around and stepped into the hair salon.

Wow. The place was like a fairy-tale ballroom, with chandeliers and everything. And it was just for doing people's hair.

Maggie was whisked into another soft chair. A second later a cup of tea was in her hand and Marcus was adjusting a wig on her head.

Her cell phone rang, and she picked it up. "What do you do if one of the burgers catches fire?" Julia cried.

"Don't panic. Happens all the time," Maggie answered. Marcus slid a plastic cap with a ton of little holes in it onto Maggie's head, then began pulling small sections of hair through each hole. "Whack the burger with a towel until it goes out. Then you have to clean the grill. It has too much grease on it. There's a scrapey thing on the shelf above it. Now get out of Dan's office before you—"

The dial tone cut her off. Maggie prayed that Julia hadn't gotten caught on the phone twice in one day.

When Maggie glanced up, she realized Marcus was staring at her as if she'd sprouted a second nose. He probably didn't have a lot of clients who toiled in the fast-food industry. Oh, well.

She closed her eyes and tried not to worry as Marcus fiddled around, achieving the perfect fit.

"Hello, gorgeous!" he finally exclaimed.

Maggie opened her eyes and stared at herself in the mirror. She didn't look like someone who'd ever eaten in a Burger Castle, let alone worked in one. Julia had told her to get the wig styled with the hair up, and Marcus had done an awesome job, making dozens and dozens of tiny braids and twining them together in a high bun on the top of her head.

Hello, rich girl, Maggie thought. She grinned. She'd definitely gotten the better end of the trade with Julia. Maybe her Sweet Sixteen wasn't going to be so awful after all.

CASTLE SPA

Italian Fango with Pretty Feet Massage $50
Seaweed Cell Fluid $50
Brush & Tone Therapy $55
Herbal Wrap $50
Dead Sea Salt Glow $50
Loofah Scrub $50
Swedish Massage $90
Aromatherapy $95
Shiatsu Therapy $95
Shampoo, Cut & Style $125
Cap Highlights* $95
Foil Highlights* $130
Permanent Body Waves* $95
Manicure $25
Full Set of Silk Wraps $75
Full Set of Fiberglass Wraps & Tips $85
Pedicure $45
Waxing from $15
Eye Treatment $65
Facial $90
Yon-Ka Facial $105

*Additional charge for long hair

Julia's face grew damp with sweat as she stood over the vat of bubbling fry oil. At least she was doing okay at this station. No disasters yet.

She stared down at the fries, watching them turn from pasty white to a perfect golden brown. When the buzzer went off, she grabbed the fry basket immediately. She didn't want the fries to be cooked one moment too long.

Julia jerked the basket out of the vat and sent a shower of hot oil arcing to her left. *It's okay,* she told herself. *It's okay. No one screamed or anything, so no one got burned.*

chapter 5

Cautiously she took a peek. Droplets of oil were scattered on the tile floor—no damage there—and on a pair of leather shoes, familiar-looking leather shoes.

Slowly Julia raised her eyes from the shoes to the face of the man wearing the shoes—Dan Paseltina, otherwise known to the employees as the big boss, and as the nutcase, and as—

"Do you know how much these shoes cost?" Dan demanded, pulling Julia out of her thoughts.

Julia emptied the fries into the warmer, then shot another look at the shoes in question. She was relieved to see they were Dr. Martens. "Eighty-five dollars?" Julia asked Dan's shoes.

"Eighty-seven ninety-two," Dan answered.

"I'll pay you for them, I promise," Julia told him. She snatched up the big metal shaker and started salting the fries. Dan just looked at her. Julia shook the shaker harder. Was he waiting for her to go get her purse right now? Oh, no! Did Maggie even have eighty-seven ninety-two in her wallet?

Finally Dan shook his head. "Just do me a favor and get your head screwed on straight, all right? I don't know what it is with all of you—you turn sixteen, and your brains start leaking out of your ears."

"Wheeler, take over the fry station. Make sure to throw out the batch of all-salt, high-blood-pressure specials Watkins just made," he called over his shoulder. "And you—" Dan turned back to Julia. "Get on register one and stay out of my sight until your shift is over."

Julia scurried out of the kitchen and over to the long row of registers. The rough polyester of her uniform scratched her legs with every step. She figured register one was at the near end of the counter, so she stepped up to it. "May I help the next person?" she asked.

A man with twin little boys—one all in blue from sneakers to baseball cap, the other all in green—rushed over to her, cutting off a teenage girl. "I'll have two Lil' Prince burgers, a King, a large Coke, and two milks," he rattled off.

Julia studied the register. There were pictures for all the menu items on the buttons, so she didn't think this could be too difficult. She was practically a straight-A student, after all. She found the buttons for the food and the drinks and hit total. "That's eight fifty-seven," she read off the register screen.

"I want fries," the blue twin announced, tugging on his father's hand.

"And a fry," the man said.

Julia found the fry buttons. "Small or large?" she asked. She glanced back toward the kitchen, hoping Dan was noticing what a good job she was doing, but he was nowhere in sight.

"Large," the man answered. Julia hit the button and hit total again. "Okay, that will be ten forty-one."

"I want onion rings instead," the blue twin said.

The man pressed his fingers against his temples. "Fine, large onion rings instead," he told Julia. She found the onion ring button and hit that. But she still had to get off the fries. She searched the register keyboard—wasn't there an erase button or a delete or something?

Julia gave a tentative smile at the guy working the register next to hers. "Uh, I don't know what's wrong with me," she said. "I can't remember what to do when I need to take an item off an order."

"You have to get the key from Dan," the guy answered, sounding sort of disgusted.

Dan. The man who had told her to stay out of his sight. Hot panic began to boil inside Julia's stomach until it felt like the french fry vat.

Calm down, she told herself in a voice that sounded strangely like her mother's. *There must be a compromise that can be negotiated here—just the way there always is at committee meetings.* Julia leaned over the counter and gave the blue twin her best smile. "The french fries are yummy. Are you sure you wouldn't like them?"

The blue twin smiled back at her and nodded. *I'm getting a handle on the working girl situation,* Julia thought. Then she realized that she hadn't actually solved her problem. Now she needed to take the onion rings off the order.

"Daddy, I'm hungry," the green twin whined. "Why is it taking so long?"

"Daddy, I'm hungry," the blue twin repeated, mocking his brother.

"Stop imitating me!" the green twin said, whine turning into a wail.

"Stop imitating *me!*" the blue twin wailed back.

"Quiet, both of you," the man begged. He nailed Julia with a hard look. "I'm getting a migraine," he told her, his words slow and deliberate. "Do you know what a migraine feels like?"

Julia shook her head.

The man leaned forward until his face was an inch away from hers. "It feels like an ice pick digging into your brain, okay? So"—he glanced at her name tag— "so, *Maggie,* I want you to do whatever you have to do to get us our food—now!"

Julia backed away, her mind filled with a very vivid image of *herself* with an ice pick in her brain. "Be right back," she mumbled. Then she ducked into the kitchen. Dan wasn't there. He wasn't in his office, either.

"He's in the john," the guy at the fry station— Wheeler—told her. "And he brought the newspaper with him, so he'll be a while."

"Don't think I won't come back there and find you!" the man yelled from the front counter.

Julia got french-fry-vat stomach again.

There was only one thing she could do. And she really did not want to do it.

Pretend you're Maggie, she told herself. *Maggie would have no problem with this.* Julia marched through the employee's-only door and into the short hallway with the bathrooms. She didn't allow herself a second's hesitation. She strode over to the men's-room door and knocked.

No one answered. Julia shifted from foot to foot. *Pretend you're Maggie,* she told herself again. She cracked open the door. "Um, excuse me, Dan?" she called. "I need the register key. The custo—"

"I don't friggin' believe this," Dan exploded from one of the stalls. "Watkins, if you're not out of this place by the time I come out of here, it's not going to be pretty."

"But the custom—"

"Go!" Dan roared. "And if you haven't patched up your brain leak by your next shift—"

"I will. I promise," Julia answered. Then she spun around, ducked back through the employees-only door, grabbed her street clothes, and ran out the side exit of Burger Castle without looking back.

She hit the sidewalk at full speed, then skidded to a stop. Julia had no idea where she was supposed to go now because she had no idea where Maggie lived. In their excitement she and Maggie had forgotten to exchange that very basic information.

Stay calm, she told herself in that voice that sounded like her mother's. *All you have to do is call Maggie and ask for her address and directions.* Julia spotted a pay phone a few feet away and headed over. She fished a quarter out of Maggie's purse and fed it into the phone, but she didn't get a dial tone. She moved down to the next phone, but it didn't have a receiver.

Suddenly cute little Brooklyn, with its short little buildings, didn't feel quite so homey anymore. She was stuck here in an unfamiliar place, surrounded by strangers, with no car and no driver in sight.

Don't be such a princess, Julia told herself. This time the voice in her head sounded more like Maggie. *There must be another pay phone in another block or so. You're in Brooklyn, not Borneo. It* is *part of the civilized world. They have Starbucks and everything.*

Julia pulled another quarter out of Maggie's purse so she'd be ready when she found the next phone. Then it hit her—she had Maggie's purse. Which meant that she probably had something with Maggie's address on it.

A little zing of self-satisfaction zipped through her. Who needed a car and driver? She pulled out Maggie's Velcro wallet and opened it.

She caught a flash of movement to her right, and she jerked up her head. A tall guy, goth in the extreme— black-purple hair, black leather vest and dog collar, black biker boots, pierced nose and eyebrow—was coming straight toward her. His eyes—brilliant green made even greener by the heavy black eyeliner—were locked on hers.

What did he want? Was he going to try and pick her up? Was he going to try and rob her? Julia shoved the wallet back into the purse and zipped the purse up tight.

"Um, my driver's going to be here any second," Julia blurted out. "He's just circling the block because he couldn't find a parking place."

The guy smirked at her, his black lipstick glistening, and Julia realized there was space for at least three cars along the curb next to them. "A bunch of cars just pulled out," she added quickly.

He peered down the street. "Maybe your driver got jacked."

Jacked. As in car jacked, Julia realized. Was this *that* kind of neighborhood?

Julia pulled her purse higher on her shoulder. She glanced up from under her eyelashes at the goth boy. Why was he just standing here?

"I'm sure it didn't get jacked," she answered. She kept her voice cool and chilly, hoping the guy would pick up on the fact that she had no interest in continuing to converse with him. "He's probably just stuck in traffic."

The guy threw back his head and laughed, the sunlight sparkling off his nose and eyebrow ring. "Maggie, you're de-evolving. The last time you pretended you were a rich girl, you were, like, seven."

He knows me. At least he knows Maggie, Julia thought. *And he has for a long time.* Muscles she hadn't even known were tense relaxed a little.

The guy looped his arm through Julia's, and all the muscles tensed right back up. *Is he Maggie's boyfriend?* she thought wildly. *Is he going to expect me to kiss him or something?*

"I almost didn't recognize you with all that hair," the guy said. "I thought you always said it was too much of a pain in the butt to deal with extensions."

"Um, I thought I should try it once. I can always hack them off if I hate it," Julia answered, pleased with her Maggie-speak.

A woman wheeling a baby carriage turned the corner. As soon as she saw them, she made a point of crossing the street. *She thinks we're freaks,* Julia thought. *Or at least she thinks he's a freak, which makes me a freak by association. I wonder what she's thinking about us. Does she think that we spend all day doing drugs or robbing liquor stores or something? Does she think—*

What do you care what she thinks? That was definitely the Maggie voice. Julia's mother always cared what people thought.

The thought of her mother made Julia cringe. If her mother and father could see her right this instant, strolling along a street in *Brooklyn,* with a guy who looked like Marilyn Manson's younger brother—

They would disown me.

Eat Like a Prince, but Pay Like a Pauper

King $2.86 Burger robed with lettuce, special sauce, and grilled onions
        $3.04 With cheese
        $3.55 With bacon and cheese

Queen $1.39 Burger robed with ketchup, pickle, and grilled onions
        $1.47 With cheese

Prince $2.72 Turkey burger robed with lettuce, ketchup, and grilled onions

Princess $2.72 Chickenwich robed with lettuce and mayonnaise

Jester $2.90 Fishwich robed with lettuce and tartar sauce

Lil' Prince Burger $.99 Junior-size burger robed with ketchup and pickle

Royal Rings	Royal Fries	Royal Cheese Fries
Small $1.34	Small $1.34	Small $1.80
Large $2.21	Large $1.84	Large $2.30

**Coke, Sprite, Root Beer, Cherry Coke, Diet Coke,
Iced Tea, Fruit Punch, Lemonade**
Small $.97   Medium $1.06   Large $1.15

Milk	Orange Juice	Coffee, Tea, Sanka
$1.29	$1.52	Small $.74
		Large $.97

Maggie opened the next door in the long hallway and peeked inside. This bedroom couldn't be Julia's. At least Maggie hoped it couldn't be. It was beautiful, but it looked like a museum exhibit or something, not that Maggie spent a lot of time in museums. There wasn't any kind of personality showing—forget about the piles of clothes and junk all over Maggie's bedroom.

She shut the door softly and tiptoed down the hall. She wasn't usually a tiptoeing kind of girl, but there was something about this place that made it feel wrong to make noise in here.

This has got to be it, Maggie thought as she reached the next door. Julia's family's apartment was huge, but it was still an apartment, not a castle or anything. And Maggie had already checked pretty much every other room. Lucky for her, Julia's 'rents weren't home yet. There was a housekeeper type in the kitchen, but otherwise Maggie had the place to herself.

"Bingo," Maggie whispered when she opened the

chapter

6

door. This was definitely the room of a princess. There wasn't much personal stuff in here, either, definitely no clutter. But a canopy bed had the place of honor in the center of the room, and Maggie just knew that was where Julia slept. Back when Maggie was a little kid, when she'd daydreamed about her mother being a glamorous actress who would swoop her out of Brooklyn and into a sparkling, magical, Hollywood world, this is the kind of bed she'd imagined she'd sleep in. But she'd given up that dream a long time ago. Pretty much around the same time she'd finally accepted that her mother was never coming back.

Maggie wandered over to the mirrored dressing table across from the bed and sat down on the flouncy upholstered chair. "Except Mom did come back," she whispered to the reflection. It felt kind of like she was talking to Julia because the girl in the mirror with the elegant hairstyle didn't look anything like Maggie. "She waited until I'd stopped wishing and hoping and dreaming. Then she came back."

The girl in the mirror's eyes looked suspiciously moist, and Maggie stood up in disgust. *Not going there,* she scolded herself.

She glanced around the room, and the canopy bed drew her like a magnet. She had to try it out.

A thrill of little-girl excitement raced through Maggie as she parted the sheer lavender drapes and climbed onto the big, soft bed. It actually smelled like lavender, a clean, classy smell.

Careful not to mess up her new hair, she snuggled into the mound of little pillows—all hearts, satin hearts, embroidered hearts, tapestry hearts, velvet hearts—and gave a long sigh of contentment. Yes, she certainly got the better end of the trading-birthdays bargain.

Maggie stared up at the canopy. "It's like being inside a cloud. No, like being wrapped in fairy wings," she murmured. She sat up fast. *Oh my God*, she thought. *My brain is starting to turn to goo. Scoz would have been rolling on the floor, busting a gut, if he could have heard me just then.*

She started to slide back off the bed, then she noticed something taped to one of the canopy's supports. She pushed herself to her knees to check it out. It was a photo of a good-looking, clean-cut guy—short dark hair, big brown eyes, wide smile, straight teeth, prepster to the max. Tyler. Had to be. Cute. Really cute. If you went for that type, which Maggie definitely didn't.

Yeah, that's why your body temperature went up a couple of degrees just looking at the picture, Maggie thought.

She ripped down the photo. Julia was never going to get

over the guy if she slept under his picture every night. *In fact, it would be doing JuJu a favor if I tore this thing into a million pieces—and then burned the pieces.* The guy had treated Julia like dog poop. And he was going to get what was coming to him, if Maggie had anything to do with it. Which, of course, she did.

Maggie started to tear the picture in half but hesitated before the rip reached Tyler's face. *I should study it a little more,* she decided. *I don't want to walk right by Tyler at the party without recognizing him.*

As if, she thought before she could stop herself. Yeah, there would probably be a lot of hotties at the party. But not all Julia's friends could be *this* gorgeous.

And hopefully all Julia's friends wouldn't be scum.

Maggie scrambled off the bed. It was time to find out exactly how big of a scum Tyler was. She bet Julia was the type who saved everything—actually Maggie was that type too—so there were probably a bunch of e-mails from Tyler saved on Julia's computer.

Now all Maggie had to do was find the computer. She knew Julia had one, but clearly it didn't fit the decor. Maggie scanned the room. She spotted a tall cupboard thingie that looked like a good hiding spot. She hurried over and swung open the doors. Yes! A top-of-the-line Apple sat there waiting for her.

Maggie slid the computer out on its rolling tray, grabbed another one of those flouncy chairs from a spot by the window—the window with the killer view of Central Park—and plopped down.

About three seconds later—thanks to a state-of-the-art modem and the password Julia had given her—she was on-line as Julia1222. The girl could use a little more imagination in the screen name department. Maggie grinned as she hit the setup menu and added a second screen name to the account —JuJuAgogo. Now that was a name that said "I'm a girl who likes fun."

Okay, now Maggie needed the old-mail folder. She clicked on the little mailbox and scanned the list of stuff that had come in to Julia. There was a whole bunch of entries from someone called T-man3.

Maggie selected the most recent one, and started to read.

To: Julia1222
From: T-man3
Re: Green, green grass
Julia,
    That "Kiss Me" song came on the radio when I was falling asleep. I guess it infiltrated my dreams or something, because all night long you and I were in a big grassy field. Maybe Sheep's Meadow in the

park? Anyway, the stars were really bright. Bright, but soft at the same time. And a lot closer than usual. Like practically touchable. And we were lying under them and kissing. Just kissing forever. Until my mom was knocking on my door, telling me I was going to be late for school.

Ty

Whoa. *Whoa.* A guy had written that to JuJu? If a guy had sent something like that to Maggie, she'd have been at his door in—

The guy who wrote that is the same guy who ground Julia's heart into pulp, Maggie reminded herself. Clearly he was a player—a top-ranked player—who knew exactly what to say to make a girl melt. Until he got bored.

Maggie clicked the next message from T-man3.

To: Julia1222
From: T-man3
Re: You
Julia,

I love typing your name. Let me type it again. Julia. Instead of the keys my fingers are touching you. Julia. Julia. Julia.

Juliajuliajuliajuliajuliajuliajuliajuliajuliajulia.

Julia.

Touching you, Julia.
Touch me, Julia.
Julia.

Maggie could almost feel the hands as she read. Warm hands.

Look, all he's saying is that he wants to touch her, Maggie told herself. Translation: Baby, I'm in the mood. *He just worded it all nice because he's a player and knows what works.* Maggie knew she had Tyler pegged. She didn't need to read any more. But she couldn't stop herself from clicking on another message from him.

To: Julia1222
From: T-man3
Re: Soul mates
Julia,

Something strange happened last night when we kissed. My soul lifted straight out of my body. And I was looking down at us. I was kissing you and watching myself kiss you at the same time.

And then your soul flew up next to mine. And our souls started kissing, the most intense kiss I've ever felt. Because it wasn't about flesh. It was about dissolving boundaries. Shared secrets. Shared life force.

Did you feel it, too? You did, didn't you? You had to. Because part of your soul is still inside me. And I know part of mine is still in you.

I think that's what people mean when they say soul mate.

Ty

Maggie clicked off the computer. No wonder Julia was such a basket case today. Tyler had made her feel like the most special girl on the planet, his frigging *soul mate*. And then he announced it was all a lie.

Well, he was going to pay. Tonight. Maggie wasn't sure exactly how, but it was a done deal.

"And I'm going to look fabulous doing . . . whatever I decide to do to him," she muttered as she headed toward the closet. "Because that will be the salt in the wound."

Maggie yanked open the closet door—and gasped. It was like a whole department store in there. Twinsets of every color. Coats of every length. Jackets of every fabric. Shoes of every style.

She checked the label on the white denim jacket closest to her. Jean Paul Gaultier. Wow. The next three labels she read were all Armani. Unbelievable. Then three Cynthia Rowley, two Richard Tyler, a couple of Romeo Gigli, and some more Armani. Maggie had never even *touched* clothes like this before.

Next came a Dolce & Gabbana crocheted granny-square sweater. It had obviously never been worn. The price tag was still on it. Maggie took a peek and jerked away her hand as if it had caught on fire.

Now she knew why she'd never come close to a Dolce & Gabbana. Talk about out of her league. That sweater . . . that *one* sweater cost almost a thousand dollars.

If the sweater cost that much, how much did the party dress cost? Maggie didn't have any trouble figuring out which dress was *the* dress. Even if she hadn't seen the swatch of material, she'd have known instantly. It was just like the canopy bed—it said princess. It would have screamed princess, but it was just too classy to raise its voice. Spaghetti straps, draped neckline, full length, small train, simple, simple, simple. No bows or froufrou. And gorgeous.

Maggie checked the label. Vera Wang. Of course. Every year, Maggie and her dad, the movie addict, watched the Oscars together. And it seemed like half the actresses walked up the red carpet in a Vera Wang gown.

Oh, man. I wish my dad could see me in this, she thought. Although she wasn't sure exactly how she was going to put it on without touching it. How did people actually wear these clothes? It was like walking around covered in hundred-dollar bills.

"Let's see how you turned out," one of those silky-smooth voices Maggie had been hearing so often today called.

Maggie turned and saw a man and a woman standing in the bedroom doorway. Mr. and Mrs. Rich People. Definitely. *It's show time,* Maggie thought.

She opened her mouth to say hi but ended up just smiling. She didn't even know what Julia called them. They didn't seem like the moms-and-pops type. Mother and Father? Mom and Dad? Sir and Ma'am?

Julia's mother walked over to Maggie and studied her for a moment. Maggie tried not to fidget. She didn't know much about the woman, but she didn't look like the type who approved of fidgeting.

Finally Julia's mother nodded. "Perfect," she said. She reached out and made a minute adjustment of the position of one of the tiny braids. "Perfect," she repeated.

"Not quite perfect," Julia's father corrected. He pulled a small box out from behind his back.

Maggie wasn't a rich girl, but even she knew that bright blue boxes with white ribbons came from

Tiffany's. Her fingers trembled as she reached out and took the present.

"For me?" she asked.

Both of Julia's parents laughed. Maggie laughed, too. Then she slid the ribbon off the box. *It's not a bomb or anything,* she told herself as she slowly, slowly pulled off the lid.

Nope, definitely not a bomb. It was a tiara. Not a big, honking one like what the queen would wear. But tiny and delicate—a circlet of silver leaves shimmering with small diamonds.

"I don't—I don't know what to say," Maggie stammered.

Julia's mother slid the tiara out of the box and carefully placed it around the bun on Maggie's head. "Thank you is always appropriate," she said.

"Thank you!" Maggie cried, forgetting to keep her voice low and controlled the way Julia did. "Thank you, thank you, thank you!"

And then both of Julia's parents put their arms around Maggie. She held on to them tight. Her dad hugged her all the time. But this was Maggie's first ever, mom-dad-daughter three-way hug. She fought back the tears threatening to fill her eyes. *Does Julia realize how lucky she is?* Maggie thought. *How crazy lucky?*

"Happy birthday," both of Julia's parents said as they pulled away.

Maggie just kept on smiling at them. She didn't think she could stop smiling if she tried.

"Sixteen years old," Julia's father said. "I can hardly believe it." He glanced at Julia's mother. "Especially when you look so young."

Julia's mother smiled at her husband and then looked back at Maggie. "This year, Julia, I'm certain you'll be invited to host a table at the Breast Cancer Awareness luncheon, which, as you know, is quite an honor," Julia's mother said. "And it's almost time for me to contact my sorority sisters from Duke and solicit recommendations. Not that there is any question of your getting in. It's only a formality."

It sounded like Julia's mother had everything in Julia's life planned out. From what she was going to be doing tonight, to next month, and even college.

Suddenly Julia's parents were talking a mile a minute about the party, and Maggie could hardly keep track of it.

". . . and Julia, when Doctor Biehl comes through the reception line, mention the article he had published in the AMA journal, would you? It was about advancements in laser eye surgery. You could just say that it was fascinating. It will put him in a good mood for the rest of the night," Julia's father was saying.

"And don't forget to tell Mrs. Wallace that she looks wonderful," Julia's mother instructed. "She had her eyes done. And I believe her chin, although she won't admit that. She doesn't want people to know she's had any work at all, but of course she wants people to notice that she's looking especially well."

Maggie nodded mutely. Although she had no clue how she was going to do what they wanted since she didn't know what these people looked like. She could just tell all the women how great they looked. But the doctor . . . well, maybe he'd just have to get in a good mood on his own.

"And Julia"—Julia's mother's eyebrows drew together ever so slightly—"make a point of chatting with Mr. and Mrs. Sanderson tonight. I want them to know that your little tiff with Tyler hasn't affected your warm feelings toward them." She made another tiny adjustment on one of Maggie's braids. "Although I still believe that when Tyler sees you tonight, the tiff will be over."

"What if I don't want it to be?" Maggie burst out. She was starting to feel frustrated. It was her—or Julia's—Sweet Sixteen. It was supposed to be this incredible night. And all her parents cared about was keeping Tyler's parents and Mrs. Whosits and Dr.

Whatevers happy. What about Julia? Didn't they care if she was happy on her own birthday?

"Don't let your pride stand in the way of taking Tyler back. I know how you feel about him," Julia's mother said, her voice growing even more silky.

"And we know how he feels about you," Julia's father jumped in. "Remember, he asked you to marry him when you were both still in Pampers."

"That was a long time ago," Maggie muttered.

"Please speak clearly," Julia's mother chided. "And you're right, it was a long time ago," she continued. "Which should remind us all how long we've been friends with the Sandersons. They've known you since you were tiny. This night is almost as important to them as it is to us."

Important because of the friendship? Or because of your business? Maggie thought.

"We know we can depend on you to be our perfect princess tonight," Julia's father said. He reached out and gave her arm a squeeze. "We know you'll make us proud. Just the way you always have."

Yeah, Julia had always made them proud—by doing exactly what they wanted her to do.

Well, tonight, *Julia* was taking orders from no one but herself.

There were three doors in the short, narrow hallway. Three closed doors. One of them had to be the door to Maggie's bedroom. But Julia wasn't sure which one.

Oh, just pick one, she ordered herself, in the voice that sounded like Maggie's. *If you pick wrong, laugh it off.* The goth guy—Julia still hadn't figured out his name—might think it was strange, but that was of no consequence.

Julia strode to the closest door on the left and pulled it open with what she hoped looked like great authority. "This is my room," she blurted out.

chapter 7

"Yeah, I guess your room is under here somewhere," the guy agreed. He stepped past her and wandered over to the bed. He sprawled out on top of it without bothering to shove over the pile of clothes. Julia could see half a bra sticking out from under his back.

So now what? Was she supposed to go over and lie next to him? Was that their usual routine—a home-alone make-out session? Or would it be more than a make-out session? The thought lowered Julia's body temperature by several degrees.

Good manners will see you through any situation, the voice of Julia's mother said calmly and clearly in Julia's head.

Oh, right, Mom! Julia thought sarcastically.

But maybe good manners could buy her a little time. "Would you like a soda or maybe a snack?" she asked politely. She tried not to stare at the boy. But he looked even stranger in Maggie's room, surrounded by ordinary objects like binders, and sweat socks, and stuffed animals, and that basketball hoop suspended practically right over his head.

He cocked his head and stared at her for a few seconds. "Like you always say, I can get it myself. I know the way to your kitchen, and my hands and feet aren't broken," he answered.

"I could make us something," she offered, not willing to give up her chance to get away from him for a few minutes.

"No, you couldn't. We don't want to be sick at your party," he answered. He shoved himself back to his feet, and Julia was so relieved to see him off the bed, she almost cheered. "I'll do it," he continued. "Although I don't see how you stay so skinny when you eat practically nonstop."

Julia backed up, in what she hoped wasn't a rude or obvious way, as he headed past her and out the door again. What she needed now was Maggie's diary—and quickly. She had to figure out (a) what the guy's name was and (b) what kind of relationship he had to Maggie.

She scanned the room, her heart thudding erratically. There was so much, so much *garbage* in here that she didn't know how Maggie even managed to get in and out. *Let's just hope we're alike in more ways than appearance,* Julia thought. She rushed over and slid open the top drawer of Maggie's desk—the drawer where Julia kept her own diary. A blue plaid notebook was jammed in back. *Yes.*

Julia pulled it free and flipped it open. She'd gotten lucky again. She started to skim. School stuff. A list of things Maggie would like to do to Dan—including making him clean the Burger Castle bathrooms with his tongue. More school stuff. A poem that seemed to be about Maggie's mother. And—there we go.

Dear JuJu,
You'll never guess who went goth—Scoz! I almost busted a gut when I saw him in Spanish. He'd

gone all out. He was even wearing makeup.
Actually, he looked kind of hot, but we're talking
Scoz. We're talking the guy who ironed his Boy
Scout uniform himself. We're talking the guy who
actually owned and wore a pocket protector.
We're talking Scoz. Enough said.

I've got a name at least, Julia thought. Sort of a name,
anyway. Whatever kind of name Scoz was. And it was
pretty clear that Scoz and Maggie weren't a couple.
Unless Maggie was one of those kinds of girlfriends
who was constantly mocking her guy. But Julia couldn't
see that. It was true that Maggie had been a bit sarcastic to Julia when they first met, but it didn't take long
for her to show her softer self.

Julia started flipping through the diary again, scanning
for the name Scoz. It came up again a few pages later.

Dear JuJu,
I don't know what I'm going to do with Scoz. He got
another piercing today. It's not that I don't think
they're cool, but if he doesn't get a grip, he's going to
be able to use himself for a spaghetti strainer or
something.

He says his goth thing has nothing to do with Lainie. But let's get real. She broke up with him. He bought himself a dog collar. It's like if he looks completely different, he won't be the same person who got hurt, which means he won't feel hurt. At least that's what I think his twisted logic is. The idiot.

I haven't said this to him—not yet—but getting dumped is the best thing that ever happened to him. (If he stops the piercing madness!) Lainie was a user. Scoz deserves so much better. I mean if I were a girl—well, of course I am a girl, but I mean a girl who isn't Scoz's buddy girl—I'd go for him.

Julia had slapped the diary closed and tossed it back in the drawer when she heard heavy footsteps coming back down the hall. A second later Scoz appeared with a tray of crackers topped with some kind of bright orange cheese substance and jalapeño peppers. He had two cans of Dr Pepper jammed under his arm.

"So did you pick out what you're wearing or what?" he asked through a mouthful of cracker. "We don't have much time."

"We don't? What time's the party?" Julia asked before she could stop herself.

Scoz rolled his eyes. "The party—like you could forget—is at eight. But we—like you could forget—have our prebirthday outing to do."

Prebirthday outing. So she was going to have to go out in public and be seen with Mr. Freak again. Julia felt a twinge of guilt at the nasty thought. It was clear from Maggie's diary that she thought Scoz was a good guy.

"Maggie. Go. Closet. Get clothes," Scoz said, doing something that sounded vaguely Tarzan-esque. Not that Julia had ever seen a Tarzan movie.

Julia obediently hurried over to the closet and swung open the door. What had Maggie been planning to wear tonight? Nothing jumped out at her as the party dress. She fingered a denim skirt.

"Oh, please," Scoz cried as he flopped down on the bed again.

"How about this?" Julia pulled out a long black skirt.

"Does it still fit? It's been two years since you flunked out of band," Scoz said.

Julia held up the skirt in front of her. "I think I can squeeze into it," she answered.

"Passable," said the goth boy, acting as if he had a

right to comment on fashion. "But what are you going to wear with it?"

Julia peered into the closet. There were T-shirts—all with slogans on them—and sweatshirts, and more T-shirts, and a baseball jersey, and a couple of denim work shirts, and a couple of ski sweaters.

"Um. Hmmm," Julia murmured. She turned to look for a dresser. But there wasn't one. "Maybe I could wear one of my dad's white shirts," she said. She hoped "dad" was what Maggie called her father.

"You'd look like a waiter," Scoz answered. He jammed two more crackers into his mouth.

He was right. If the skirt wasn't black, she could get away with it. But the skirt was black.

Julia swept her eyes across the clothes scattered on the floor and bed. She didn't see any possibilities. There was still time for a little last minute shopping. Except if Maggie'd had the money to buy something new, wouldn't she have already?

"What about this?" Julia plucked a short black dress out of a pile in the corner. It was nothing fancy, but it was certainly sexy.

Scoz laughed. "Like you'd wear that. I had no idea you even *owned* a dress."

"Why not?" Julia answered. She'd always loved the

short, trendy dresses she'd seen girls wearing around town, only her mother had never let her have one. She thought they were tacky.

But her mother wasn't going to be at the party. And it might be kind of fun to dress sexy for once. Julia suddenly felt needle pricks of nervousness on the skin she was thinking about baring.

"You might actually look like a girl is why not," Scoz answered.

"I always look like a girl," Julia protested. Maggie definitely hadn't looked like a boy in her jeans and T-shirt today.

"Yeah, but not a, you know . . ." Scoz got very busy chewing. "I guess I should shut up."

A knock sounded on the open door. Julia looked over and saw a man standing there. She assumed it had to be Maggie's dad, although the two of them didn't look anything alike.

"Scoz, I need a little time alone with Maggie," he said. He looked uncomfortable.

Scoz tossed Julia one of the sodas and headed out. "I'll watch the tube until you're ready," he called over his shoulder.

Maggie's father shut the door behind him, and Julia's heart began its stop-and-start beating again. She didn't know Maggie's father at all, but she could tell that something was wrong.

"Mags, baby, I don't know what to say. I should have told you before—" He pulled a stack of envelopes out from behind his back. "Your moth—Annette, she wrote to you a few times over the years. I've been thinking about it for a long time, but I just couldn't . . ." His voice trailed off.

Julia's fingers trembled as she reached out and took the envelopes from Maggie's father. *Maggie needs to be here right now,* she thought. *This is huge. This is monumental.* Julia had no idea how to act, what to say.

She didn't get any help from the voice that sounded like her mother.

Say what you think Maggie would want to say, Julia told herself. She forced herself to look Maggie's father in the eye, because, although she didn't know Maggie all that well, she knew Maggie was the confrontational type. "You had these letters all these years and you're just giving them to me now?" she demanded.

Maggie's father sat down on the side of the bed and patted the spot next to him. Julia shook her head, and he seemed to accept that. He stared down at his hands for a long moment, then he returned his gaze to hers. "I didn't think she deserved you," he said slowly, as if he was choosing each word with careful consideration. "She left you. Why should she get to be a part of your life?" His words came faster now. "Why should she get a piece of that joy? It just isn't fair."

Julia could hear anger in his voice, but underneath that, anguish. She sat down next to him and knotted her hands in Maggie's faux-zebra-skin bedspread. "Shouldn't who has a part in my life be my decision?" she asked, the question coming out more gentle than she'd intended.

"When you were five? No. When you were eleven? Maybe," Maggie's father answered. "Now . . ." He looked down at his hands again.

"Now?" Julia prompted.

"You're growing up." He ran his hand over his bald head. "Hell, you're grown up. The same age as Annette when she had you. I decided I shouldn't be thinking for you anymore." He stood up. "Besides, Annette's going to be at the party." He gave a pained smile. "I figured she might tell you about them, and if she told you before I did, I didn't know if you'd ever forgive me."

Is this really how Maggie's father talks to her? Julia thought. He was acting as if they were equals, not as if he were an all-knowing, all-powerful parent-god. Did Maggie know how incredibly lucky she was to have this?

"I don't know what to say. I don't know what to feel," Julia answered. She could hardly wrap her mind around it. Maggie thought her mother had abandoned her, but her mother had been trying to be in touch after all. This was world shattering.

"Just read the letters, and then we'll talk as much as you want." He stood up fast. "I haven't even read them myself." He hurried to the door, then glanced over his shoulder. "With your hair like that, you look exactly like her." Before Julia could reply, he was gone.

She stared at the letters in her hands. She didn't know if she should read them or not. They were incredibly personal—even if they only talked about the weather. But something in the letters might come up when she talked to Maggie's mother at the party.

She spotted a phone on the floor, snatched it up, and dialed her cell phone number. It was busy. And Scoz was waiting.

Maggie said it was okay to go through her stuff, Julia thought. She hesitated a moment longer, then she opened the top envelope, careful not to tear it. Inside was a birthday card with a poodle in a tutu on the front. Underneath the poodle were the words *To My Darling Daughter on her Fifth Birthday.*

Julia opened the card. It had been signed *Love,*

Mommy, but there was no additional message. Julia returned the card to its envelope and placed the envelope on the bottom of the stack. Then she opened the next one. It was another birthday card. This one had a kitten wearing a party hat. The words *To My Special Daughter on her Sixth Birthday* were spelled out in pink glitter. Julia peeked inside. Another *Love, Mommy.*

There were cards for the seventh, eighth, and tenth birthdays, too. Julia wondered what happened to the one for nine. Maybe after four years of getting no response to her cards, Julia's mother had been too discouraged to send one.

Or maybe she just forgot.

Julia slid open the next envelope and found another birthday card. But inside this one was a letter.

Dear Maggie,

Is that even your name? It's the name your father and I chose when I was pregnant with you. He pressed his ear against my stomach and insisted he heard a little voice crying, "I'm Maggie!" He wouldn't even think about choosing a boy's name after that, even though we told the doctor we didn't want to know if you were a boy or a girl until you came out.

Somehow I can't imagine your father calling you by another name. Although maybe I'm wrong. Maybe that memory, that memory of choosing your name, is one he wanted to forget.

Oh, Maggie. I can hardly believe you're eleven years old today. You probably think you're too old to need a mother, especially a mother like me, a disappearing non-mother. But this is really the beginning of the time when you'll need a mother most. And that's why I'm writing. If you need me for anything—<u>anything</u>—I want you to call me. My number is 530-555-1307. I'm still at the same address as I have been for the last five years. I'm always afraid to move. I'm afraid the day I do, that's the day a letter will come from you. I'm not saying that to make you feel guilty. I just want you to know that I'm here. There's so much I want to say to you. So much to try to explain. But I don't think it's fair to lay anything more on you unless you tell me that you want to hear it.

Love, Mom

Oh God, Julia thought. Her mother hated that expression, but it was the only thing that came into her mind. *Oh God. Poor Maggie. Poor Maggie's mom.*

Julia opened the next envelope. Another birthday

card with only a *Love, Mom* and a phone number. The next two cards had *Love, Mom*s, too, and the same number. The ink on the inside of the card for Maggie's fourteenth birthday was smudged, as if it had gotten wet.

The last envelope felt a little thicker, and Julia found another letter inside. She closed her eyes for a moment, not sure if she could bear to read it. Then she opened them and began.

Dear Maggie,

I've always thought about you every day. But now I find that I think about you almost every hour. You're fifteen now, the age that I was when I fell in love with your father, the age I was when I got pregnant with you. (Something I will never, ever regret.)

There's so much I wish someone would have told the fifteen-year-old me. My own mother died when I was eleven—did you know that? I don't know if you know anything about me. Do you even know my name? My name is Annette Watkins. I never changed it back after your father and I got divorced.

There's so much I wish I could tell you. But you don't know me. And although it breaks my heart, I don't know you. And the things I want to say aren't things that can be said in a letter.

How would you feel if sometime ~~░░░░░░░░░░░░░░░░░░~~ ~~░░░░░░░░░~~

Have a wonderful year, my darling fifteen-year-old daughter. Don't try to grow up too fast. And remember, if you need me or even if you don't, I'm here. 530-555-1307.

Love, Mom

Julia slowly refolded the letter and returned it to the envelope. *What am I going to say to this woman tonight?* she thought. She'd been sure it would be so easy—a little polite chitchat, the kind she'd made a million times with friends of her parents.

But chitchat wouldn't do it.

Julia knew what Maggie would want her to do. Or at least she knew what Maggie *wouldn't* want her to do. Maggie wouldn't want Julia to do or say anything that would encourage Maggie's mother to try to make a place for herself in Maggie's life.

But after reading these letters . . . would Julia be able to push Maggie's mother away?

95

dad me nobody

Maggie heard a faint crackling sound, then the voice of Julia's father filled the room. "Julia, your driver is here to take you to the party."

An intercom. They lived in an apartment so big, they needed an intercom. Unbelievable.

Maggie spotted the small intercom box near the canopy bed and hurried over to it—as well as she could hurry in her long gown and strappy Manolo Blahnik shoes.

She found the talk button and pressed it. "I'll be right there," she answered. She didn't get the driver thing. She'd just assumed she and the parents would be going over together. And anyway—she took a glance at the clock on the mantel over the fireplace—the party wasn't supposed to start for a couple of hours. *I guess that's why Julia's mom was so insistent that I get ready so early,* Maggie thought. Maybe her mother wasn't quite so anal as Maggie'd assumed.

She picked up the tiny beaded bag off the bedside table, took a deep breath, and headed out. Before she

chapter

8

stepped into the massive, high-ceilinged living room she took another deep breath.

But the moment she entered the room, all the air she'd pulled into her lungs got sucked right back out.

She'd thought Tyler looked incredible in the picture she'd found. But in the flesh . . . dressed in a tux . . . Maggie didn't even have the words to describe him. Her reaction was beyond words. It was all about sizzling neurons sending emergency signals through her heart. *Want that! Want that now!*

This is the player, Maggie reminded herself. *This is the guy who slimed Julia. This is the guy who you plan to destroy . . . somehow.*

Her brain was dishing out the logic. But her heart wasn't having any. *Want that! Want that! Want that!* it insisted.

Maggie jerked her eyes away from Tyler and over to Julia's parents' smiling faces. Smiles that said "the merger is on." Had they arranged this whole thing?

"I told you we should have asked her if it was okay for me to show up here," Tyler mumbled.

"She's delighted to see you," Julia's mother answered. "You know Julia. She can't speak when she's happy."

They were both talking as if she wasn't there. Maggie

had the feeling Julia got a lot of that. "It seems pointless to say anything," Maggie told Tyler and Julia's mother. "You two are doing fine on your own."

Julia's mother's eyebrows raised ever so slightly.

"How about some pictures before you two leave?" Julia's father jumped in. He reached for the camera on the coffee table.

"We have to get one of Tyler putting on the corsage," Julia's mother agreed, her silky voice extra sweet.

It's like someone burped and everyone's trying to pretend that they didn't hear it, Maggie thought. *As if it's so—*

Then her brain started to sputter, all thoughts dying out, as Tyler stepped toward her. He opened a plastic box and pulled out a knot of pale pink rosebuds, then looked at her for a long moment, as if waiting for an answer to an unspoken question.

Whatever he saw on Maggie's face must have seemed like a yes because he reached out and gently took her right hand in his. Julia's father's camera started to click as Tyler slid the wrist corsage into place.

Maggie hoped he couldn't feel her hand trembling. She couldn't believe her hand *was* trembling. But the brush of Tyler's fingers against the thin skin on the underside of her wrist was devastating. She could feel that touch all the way to her knees.

At least I'm still able to stand up, she thought over the buzzing in her brain, which was only now coming back to life. *At least I didn't end up with my butt on the rug.* That wouldn't have been a photo for the album.

"You ready to go?" Tyler asked.

Maggie nodded. She didn't trust herself to speak. Not when Tyler was standing so close, not when every breath she managed to take was scented with the spicy smell of Tyler's soap mixed with the smell of Tyler's skin.

Julia's mother handed Tyler a floor-length coat. To Maggie it looked elegant enough to be worn as an evening gown. Tyler moved behind her. Maggie could feel his warm breath on her neck. The sensation was so distracting that it took her a moment to realize he was waiting for her to slip her arms into the sleeves.

She missed the right sleeve once and the left sleeve twice but finally managed to get the coat on. Tyler moved from behind her to her right side, not touching her, but so near, she could feel the heat of his body soaking into hers even through her coat.

No, wait. That was impossible, her brain argued. But her body knew what it knew. Her whole right side felt degrees hotter than her left side, and her skin felt somehow alive. As if it had its own intelligence. As if it was having some kind of secret conversation with Tyler's skin. *Want that! Want that now!*

Maggie caught a questioning glance from Tyler. Then she realized he had his arm crooked toward her. How long had he been waiting for her to slip her hand through?

Doesn't matter, she told herself as she took Tyler's arm, Julia's father's camera clicking again. It was good not to seem too eager. To let the player know that his games weren't going to work anymore.

The skin of Maggie's left hand gibbered away, thrilled to have made direct contact with Tyler's body—even though the contact was through several layers of clothes. Maggie tried to ignore it.

"See you at the party," Tyler told Julia's parents. Maggie forced a smile at them as Tyler led her toward the foyer. The private penthouse elevator was waiting for them—no waiting, no crowds. They stepped inside, the door slid shut, and they were alone.

Maggie smiled at Tyler. He smiled back, a dimple appearing in one cheek. Of course. He was the dimple type. She drummed her fingers against her thigh. "So is Elena meeting us at the party, or are we picking her up?" she asked, her voice soft and sweet—she'd picked up a few tricks in her brief stay among the Manhattan rich.

"Elena?" Tyler repeated. His Adam's apple started working frantically in his throat, but that was the only indication Maggie's question had gotten to him.

"Yeah. I heard she's going to be wearing a dress that shows butt cleavage," Maggie answered, keeping her tone conversational. "I'm sure you can't wait to get yourself an eyeful of that."

Tyler pulled his arm away from Maggie, and her skin let out a wail of protest. "I don't know what you're talking about," he said, his voice a little too loud.

Maggie raised her eyebrows ever so slightly, imitating Julia's mother's did-I-hear-a-burp expression. Tyler's jaw tensed. His mouth opened as if he were about to speak but then snapped closed.

Maggie allowed her eyebrows to raise a fraction higher. Tyler shifted slightly from foot to foot. When the elevator door silently slid open, he looked relieved. He rushed across the lobby's polished wood floor and yanked open the door before the doorman could get it.

Maggie slowly made her own way across the lobby. What? She was supposed to be so thrilled by whatever kind of car Tyler had that she was supposed to forget all about Elena? Dream on.

Her body started its want-that-want-that-now chant as she slipped past Tyler, brushing lightly against him. She struggled to ignore it.

And she struggled to keep any sign of pleasure off her face when she saw the white stretch limo parked out front. Who would have ever thought Maggie Watkins would be riding in a car like that?

"It's great, huh?" Tyler exclaimed. He rushed over to the limo and opened the door for her before the chauffeur could get it.

Maggie ran her gaze over the long, gleaming car as she approached it. Finally she let her eyes meet Tyler's. "I guess when you have two dates, you need a big car," she commented. Then she slid inside. Oh, man. Wouldn't her dad love to see his baby girl right now, snuggling into a limo's leather interior. It was like a little living room back there. The seats were more like sofas—two of them facing each other with a table in between. And there was a mini-bar and a TV.

"I don't know what you heard about Elena, but whatever it was was just rumors, okay?" Tyler said as he climbed into the limo. He hesitated, then sat down across from her instead of next to her.

Maggie was glad he had. It would be easier to deal with him if he kept his distance.

"Rumors?" Maggie repeated. She waited, wanting to give Tyler a little more rope to hang himself with.

"Yeah," Tyler answered, leaning toward her. "You know how everyone at school yaps." He snapped his thumb and fingers together a few times to indicate yapping mouths.

"It's true. There are always a million rumors flying around," Maggie agreed. She noticed some of the tension ease out of Tyler's neck and shoulders. She gave him a moment to enjoy himself, then went in for the kill. "So when you told me that I bored you—" Maggie tried to remember exactly what Julia had said in the bathroom. "That when you were with me, you were always thinking about how soon you could dump me so you could hang with your buds—when you said that, it was just a rumor? When you broke up with me, it was just a *rumor?*"

Maggie watched Tyler's face carefully, but other than a slight flaring of the nostrils, his expression didn't change. *He's good,* she thought. *But not as good as me. I'm taking this boy down.*

Tyler slumped back and leaned his head on the top of the leather seat. He scrubbed his face with his fingers. "You ever have someone push you so hard to do something that you don't want to do it? Even if you *do* want to do it?" he asked without looking at her.

Maggie didn't answer. She wanted to hear more, and she thought if she stayed quiet, she would.

"It's like you and me," Tyler said, talking to the limo ceiling. "My parents and your parents have been hurling us at each other for always. The perfect couple. Yadda, yadda, yadda. I just got so sick of it. They control practically my whole life. I couldn't take them controlling who I go out with. Not anymore."

"So to make it easier on me, you didn't tell me the truth. You decided it would be better if you told me I was boring," Maggie shot back.

It's not that she didn't sympathize with the guy—a little. She would hate feeling like a puppet getting jerked here and there. But what Tyler did to Julia was wrong, no matter what the reason behind it.

"Yeah," Tyler admitted, finally looking at Maggie again. "Was I a total weenie or what? And the stupidest part is that just to get back at my parents, I gave up something I really wanted—you."

In one smooth motion he was on the seat beside her, his arm wrapped around her shoulders. "I'm not good at saying things out loud—that's why I send you all those e-mails. But I really do think we're soul mates, Julia. Can't you feel it? Can't you feel our souls

105

twining around each other? They want to be together."

Want that! Want that now! Now! Now! Now! Maggie's body insisted. Maggie jumped up and hit the button that opened the sunroof. "I think we need a little fresh air," she muttered. But what she really needed was to get her body away from Tyler's. She climbed up on the table between the two seats and leaned out of the limo.

They were driving along one of the roads that ran through Central Park. Off in the distance she could see a group of trees covered in tiny white lights. She had to give it to Tyler. He knew how to do romance. But that was to be expected. Romance was the tool of the player.

Except was he a player? The thought jumped uninvited into Maggie's head and refused to leave.

He could have been telling her the truth. He could have just gotten wigged out by his parents trying to run his life. Maybe he really did love Julia. Those e-mails—whoa. They were either from an extreme player . . .

Or from a guy in love.

"Is it okay if I come up?" Tyler asked from below.

Maggie's heart and brain were more in agreement than they had been all night. Her heart said, *Yes, yes, yes!* And her mind said, *Maybe.*

"Okay," she answered.

A few moments later he stepped up beside her and

handed her a glass of champagne. "Happy birthday," he said, and they clicked glasses. Tyler gave her the dimple smile. "Sweet sixteen and never been—"

"We've kissed lots of times," Maggie interrupted. Just saying the word *kiss* started her lips tingling. *Want that! Want that now!*

"But not since we broke up," Tyler answered.

Julia wants to get back together with him, Maggie reminded herself. *I can help her. If I kiss him, it will be what Julia would want me to do.*

Maggie leaned toward Tyler, just a fraction of an inch. That's all it took. An instant later both their champagne glasses were exploding on the street, Tyler's hands were on Maggie's waist, her hands were in his hair, and they were kissing as if they'd been starving for the taste of each other.

WHAT IS THE MOST ROMANTIC THING YOU HAVE EVER SEEN?

"My husband making me cinnamon toast while wearing the fuzzy bunny slippers our kids got him for Father's Day."—Vivian Anderson, supervisor, Parks Dept.

"I was jogging in Central Park, and this huge white limo drove past. Two high school kids were leaning through the sunroof, kissing. And that kiss . . . it was as if they were the only two people alive. Just flying through the night with all these little white lights in the trees around them."—Becky Loiacono, CPA

"Bogie putting Ingrid Bergman on the plane in Casablanca."—Mike Gaida, TV ad sales rep

Julia heard a quick double knock, then Scoz called to her through the door, "Your birthday's going to be over before we leave the house if you don't hurry up."

"Um, you can come in," she called back. "I guess," she added under her breath. She peered at herself in the long mirror attached to the inside of Maggie's closet door. The slinky black dress had seemed like a good idea, but she'd never shown so much leg in her life.

"You look amazing," Scoz said.

Julia turned around, and her heart gave a hard thump. Scoz just had that effect on her. He was so . . . freaky. Another word that her mother wouldn't approve of. But *freaky* described him perfectly.

Just imagine him with a pocket protector, she told herself, the voice in her head sounding only like her. Not her mother. Not Maggie.

Julia squinted at Scoz, trying to picture a pocket protector and a bunch of pens, including a pink highlighter, sticking out of his leather vest. She added a pair of thick glasses held together with tape for good measure. *Much less freaky and creepy,* she thought with a smile.

"What?" Scoz asked. He ran his fingers through his black-purple hair, looking self-conscious.

"Nothing," Julia said quickly. "I was just thinking that you look amazing, too." She couldn't prevent a giggle from escaping her.

Scoz's face turned grim. "Do I amuse you?" he asked menacingly. "Do you see me as some kind of clown? Is that it? I amuse you?" He took a step toward her. Julia took a step away. Scoz had just crossed the line from freaky into scary. She tried to hold on to her image of the pocket protector and glasses but couldn't. "Answer the question. Do I amuse you?" he insisted.

He took another step closer, green eyes intent on her face. Julia took another step away. "Uh, no. Of course not."

Scoz grinned. "I see my tough-guy act is getting better. I actually wigged you out that time." He turned around, picked up her jean jacket from the bed, and threw it at her.

Julia grabbed for it but was too slow. *He was just kidding,* she thought as she retrieved the coat from the floor, feeling like an imbecile. "Yeah, funny," she mumbled as she shrugged on the coat.

"You can come up with a better comeback than that," Scoz shot back as he led the way out of her room, down the hall, and over to the front door. "Mr. Watkins, we're leaving for the birthday ritual," he called.

Ritual. That was not a word Julia was entirely comfortable with. Especially coming out of the mouth of a boy wearing leather and black lipstick.

"See you at the party," Maggie's father called back. His voice sounded a little *off*, even to Julia, who hardly knew the man. *He's probably dreading tonight as much as Maggie was or almost as much,* Julia thought as she and Scoz stepped outside.

She wasn't exactly looking forward to the party herself. She didn't know how she was going to get through talking to Maggie's mother. And besides that, there were all Maggie's friends to worry about. Maggie's friends were probably all totally cool. They'd be expecting Maggie to be fun. Which meant Julia should act fun, but what did that mean, exactly?

Why couldn't Maggie have asked me to take a test for her? she thought as she and Scoz walked down the cracked, uneven sidewalk, heading Julia had no idea where. *Or why couldn't Maggie have asked me to take her place at some kind of charity function where all I'd have to do is smile and be polite? I'm good at that. But if I just smile*

and act polite tonight, everyone is going to think I'm stupid and boring.

"You have the weirdest expression on your face," Scoz commented. "What are you thinking about?"

"What am I thinking about?" Julia repeated, taken aback. Tyler never asked her what she was thinking about. When she was quiet, he was more than happy to fill up the silence with descriptions of movie plots, and jokes he'd heard, and how he was planning to change his weight-lifting program.

"Yeah. You've been kind of out of it all day. Is something going on?" Scoz asked.

Julia caught a man mowing his lawn giving Scoz a disgusted look. No, not just Scoz. Both of them. She gave the man her best company smile to show him that she at least was normal. He didn't look impressed.

"If you don't tell me right now, I'm going to lie down right here on the sidewalk until you do," Scoz threatened.

Julia was pretty sure he'd actually do it. He obviously wasn't worried about making a spectacle out of himself. And maybe it would help to tell someone else what was going on—at least part of it. *Scoz is strange, but he's Maggie's friend,* Julia reminded herself.

Scoz started to lower himself to the ground.

"No, don't!" Julia yelped, shooting a worried look at the lawn-mowing man. "I'll tell."

Scoz straightened up.

Julia studied the little tufts of grass pushing up through the cracks in the sidewalk. "I found out that my . . . that my mother is coming to the party tonight," Julia explained.

"Oh, man. I don't know what to say," Scoz answered after a pause. "It's like there's been a cave-in in my brain." He reached out and grabbed her hand. "Are you okay? How did this all happen?"

"I'm actually not okay," Julia admitted. She resisted the impulse to pull her hand away. It was too bizarre to be holding hands with a guy wearing nail polish. "I have no idea what to say to her. She left me when I was a baby, and I thought she wanted nothing to do with me. But now I find out she's been sending me birthday cards I never got because my father never gave them to me. So she has been thinking about me, and now I don't know how I'm supposed to feel. Am I still supposed to hate her? Am I supposed to forgive her because of a few cards? Am I supposed to ignore her at the party? Am I supposed to run up and hug her? Am I supposed to—"

"Wait. Wait. I can't keep up with all the questions,"

Scoz said. They turned the corner, and Scoz started down the concrete steps leading to the subway.

The subway. Julia's parents never let her ride the subway. Suddenly it didn't feel quite so bad holding Scoz's big, warm hand.

"Okay, here's what I think," Scoz said, pausing at the bottom of the steps. "I think you shouldn't try to decide how you feel until you see your mom. You have a dead-on bull meter. Talk to her, hear what she has to say. Check the meter. Then you'll know what you want to do. And whatever you do—tell her to get lost, tell her you want to see her again, whatever—it will be the right thing."

He sounded so confident in her. Or in Maggie, really. "How can you be so sure?" Julia asked.

"I am the great and powerful Scoz," he answered. "I know all." He let go of her hand and pulled a yellow card out of the pocket of his black leather pants. "You need a new MetroCard?" he asked.

"Maybe. I—let me look." Julia pulled open Maggie's purse and fumbled with her wallet. It took a minute, but she found one of the cards. "Okay. I'm ready."

Scoz shook his head. He took the wallet out of Julia's hands, put it back in her purse, and zipped it. "And you're the one who's always lecturing me on not showing my wallet in the subway," he said. He walked over to the closest turnstile, swiped his card through the slot, and stepped through.

Julia did the same—although it took her four swipes to get a "go" from the machine.

"How's your dad taking it—your mom showing up?" Scoz asked as they waited for the train to arrive.

"He's not doing so—" Julia stopped, her attention riveted on a rat eating a piece of trash on the subway tracks below the platform. Was this normal? She tried not to look as disgusted as she felt.

Scoz followed her gaze. "You know what they say about rats—pigeons with two extra feet. I don't know why you hate them so much. So anyway, your dad?"

"I think he's afraid of what will happen." She kept her eyes on Scoz so she wouldn't risk another rat sighting. "I think maybe he's afraid things will change between the two of us. I don't even know why I'm saying that."

"I know why," Scoz told her. "It's the bull meter. You get what's going on with people." He shouted the last few words to be heard over the roar of the train as it pulled into the station.

They stepped into the closest car. There were no empty seats—until two middle-aged women saw Scoz.

They got up and hurried as far from him as they could get without actually changing cars. Scoz and Julia took their seats.

"Aren't I scary," Scoz joked. "I'd tell them to come back and sit down, but they might faint or something."

Amazing. He really didn't seem to care that people found him frightening. Or that he was constantly getting stared at. It was mind-boggling to Julia. She'd spent her whole life trying to follow the rules, do what her parents expected, to make nice. Who knew you could just decide you didn't care what anyone else thought?

"Does it ever bother you?" Julia asked as they sped through a tunnel, the lights in the car flickering. She jerked her chin toward the women who'd run away from Scoz.

"I figure if people are stupid enough to judge me on how I look, they deserve what they get," Scoz said. Julia heard an undercurrent of bitterness in his voice, and what Scoz called her bull meter went off. It's not that Julia thought Scoz was lying, exactly. But something else was going on.

"Are you talking about them . . . or are you talking about Lainie?" Julia asked, remembering the name of Scoz's ex from Maggie's diary. She never would have asked that question if she hadn't been playing Maggie. It was definitely nosy and borderline rude. But she was curious, and she figured if Maggie wanted to ask, she'd ask.

Scoz gave her an annoyed look. Julia just raised her eyebrows—something she'd picked up from her mother.

"I guess I'm still annoyed that Lainie seemed perfectly happy when we were hanging out alone but got all critical when her friends made comments about my clothes and all that garbage," Scoz admitted.

"But you still want her back," Julia said, thinking about Tyler.

A harsh bark of laughter escaped from Scoz's throat. "Yeah, I want her back. But only because I'm an idiot. I'm hoping it will pass." He stood as the train jolted to a stop.

Julia stood too. *Guess it's time to find out what this ritual is.* She didn't feel quite as nervous about it as she had when they'd started out.

"I can smell the hot dogs already," Scoz exclaimed as they climbed off the train. He grabbed her hand again. "Come on." He started to run, pulling her behind him through the turnstile and up the stairs and across the street—to the Coney Island amusement park. Julia was sure that's what it had to be, even though she'd never

117

been there. She'd begged to go when she was a little girl but had been told it was much too seedy, and besides it was in Brooklyn.

She tried to take in everything as they ran—the row of carnival games, the kiddie rides, the arcade.

"You want to stop and see the world's largest rat?" Scoz yelled as they flew past a large cage draped with a black velvet cloth.

Julia gave him her answer—by whacking him on the back of the head, Maggie style. Scoz veered to the left, then came to a halt in front of a hot dog stand. "Two dogs with onions and chili, and two large cheese fries, and two large pink lemonades," he said breathlessly.

"There's going to be food at the party," Julia reminded him, her voice coming out more prim than she'd meant it to.

"We have to eat it," Scoz told her. He paid the man behind the counter and took a huge bite of the dog. "It's part of the ritual."

What could she do? It was part of the ritual. Julia took a tiny bite of the hot dog, trying not to think about exactly what was in it. "This is amazing," she said. It really was. She took a bigger bite.

"Come on," Scoz urged. "We don't have much

time." He rushed to the next food stand and bought two green cotton candies. Julia had to practically swallow the rest of her dog whole to free up a hand. She alternated the sweet fluffy stuff with the greasy fries as they headed to the ticket booth. It was a surprisingly good combination.

She smiled when she thought how nervous she'd been about the ritual. Who knew all it involved was a ton of yummy junk food? Stuff she *never* got to eat. She could definitely deal with this.

Scoz bought a strip of tickets. "It's Cyclone time," he announced. And they were running again. Past the log ride, past the fortune-teller, past the freak show tent—and over to a huge roller coaster.

"Th-this is part of the ritual?" she stammered, forgetting that she should know exactly what the ritual was.

"Shhh. I'm counting," Scoz answered. "We have to let four more people go ahead of us. Then we'll be in the first car."

Julia took a long, long drink of her pink lemonade. How was she going to get out of this? She lowered her cup and stared up at the first hill of the coaster. She couldn't go up there. She'd die if she went up there.

A man and a girl who looked about ten years old joined the line. A moment later a twenty-something couple stepped up behind them.

"This is going to be perfect," Scoz said happily as he guided her into the line.

"Scoz, I don't know if I can . . ." Julia let her words trail off.

"If you can what?" he asked.

Julia knew there was no way out. She had agreed to be Maggie, and this was part of the deal. It was worth it not to have to see Tyler and Elena slow dancing at Julia's own party, she reminded herself. She shot another look up at the coaster. *If you die, you'll never have to see Tyler or Elena ever again,* she told herself, trying to focus on the bright side.

Scoz took the empty cheese fry container out of her hand and the half-empty pink lemonade cup. He tossed them in the trash as they headed past. "We're up," he said as the coaster pulled up in front of the line.

Julia studied the faces of the people getting off. They all seemed fine. Alive, at least. She reached out and grabbed Scoz's arm with both hands. He looked surprised but didn't say anything, even when she refused to release him as they climbed into their seats, Julia in front of Scoz with his legs alongside hers.

The woman running the coaster stepped up and snapped the safety bar into place. There was no turning back now. Julia squeezed her eyes shut. *Pretend you're still in the loading area,* she told herself as the coaster started up the first hill.

But even her imagination wasn't strong enough to block out the click, click, click as they ascended and the force pushing her back against Scoz's chest.

The click, click, click stopped. The silence was worse than the sound, because it meant—

"Ahhhhhhhhhhh!" Before Julia could complete the thought, they were flying down. Her stomach was in her throat, and she was screaming, screaming as loud as she could. She'd never screamed like that before and it felt—wonderful.

"You've got to put up your hands," Scoz shouted in her ear. Julia didn't hesitate. She let go of his jacket, threw her hands in the air, and screamed again. She didn't stop screaming until they pulled back into the loading area.

"That was fantastic," she cried as she climbed out of the car. Her body flooded with joy—joy for having been brave enough to do it, for having loved it, for having screamed her lungs out. Her legs wobbled as she took her first steps back on the ground. "I'm still in the air!"

she exclaimed as Scoz grabbed her arm to steady her. "It was so—I'm so—"

Suddenly her stomach twisted, her eyes opened wide, and then she threw up, spattering pieces of partially digested hot dog all over the ground. "Oh my God, I'm so sorry," she told Scoz. "I'm so sorry."

How completely horrifying. How humiliating. She could feel people staring. She'd just done something so disgusting. They all must think she was so, so . . . and Scoz, who knew what he was thinking? He had to be wishing he was a million miles away from her. Tyler would have been as far away from her as he could get. "I'm really sorry, Scoz."

"Stop apologizing," Scoz told her. He led her out of the way of the people getting off the coaster, then he pulled a bandanna out of his pocket. He gently wiped the flecks of vomit off her mouth.

"Don't do that," she cried. She tried to pull the bandanna out of his hands. "That's so gross. How can you stand it? You can just go sit on one of the benches over there. I'll go to the bathroom and clean up and then meet you."

"Calm down. It's just puke," Scoz answered. He finished wiping her face. "Do you want a 7UP or some water or something? Or will that just make it worse?"

"How can you even stand here talking to me?" Julia blurted out. "Everybody is staring at us."

Scoz shrugged. "Who cares? There's nobody here who hasn't done something equally embarrassing." He pushed her hair out of her face, then he took her chin between his thumb and forefinger and forced her to look up at him. "Nobody," he repeated.

"That's impossible," Julia answered.

"Nope. It's true. I told you, I'm the great and powerful Scoz. I know all," he insisted. "That guy over there?" Scoz nodded toward a guy in a Mets T-shirt. "He wet the sleeping bag at camp—when he was a *counselor*."

Julia gave a snort of laughter. She couldn't help herself.

Scoz smiled. He let go of her chin and took her by the arm. "And that girl, the one trying to win that stuffed panda?" he said as they strolled back the way they'd come. "She laughed so hard that she blew orange soda out of her nose. That would have been bad enough, but it sprayed all over the term paper of this guy she had a crush on."

Julia giggled. She could easily imagine it.

"You two want a picture?" a guy in an enormous top hat called out.

"Yeah," Scoz answered. He lowered his voice so only

Julia could hear him. "I never want to forget the day you puked on my shoes." They both smiled, and the guy's camera clicked.

Julia glanced down. To her horror, there was a piece of hot dog still stuck to one of Scoz's boots. "Do you have a napkin? I'll clean it off for you," she said.

"No way. I'm leaving it. I look extra scary now," he told her.

The guy in the top hat hurried over, and Scoz paid him for the Polaroid stuck in a little cardboard frame. Julia leaned close to Scoz so she could study it. She could hardly believe the girl in the picture was her. Was that really Julia Anastasia Reed-Prescott grinning at a freaky goth guy? A freaky sweetheart of a goth guy with the greenest eyes she'd ever seen?

Julia ran her finger lightly over the photo. Yes, it was definitely her. "Can I keep this?" she asked Scoz.

WHAT IS THE MOST ROMANTIC THING YOU HAVE EVER SEEN?

"I went to a wedding last weekend, and the couple who had been married the longest got a spotlight dance. They'd been together for fifty-five years, so they'd been together almost three times as long as they'd been apart."
—Elizabeth Coffey, veterinarian

"A young lady threw up after she rode on the Cyclone roller coaster. And her boyfriend wiped her mouth and said something to make her laugh. It was absolutely the sweetest thing."—Tess Balogh, Coney Island fortune-teller

Maggie's mouth ached from smiling. She glanced down the row of people in the reception line—still about twenty-five to meet and greet. Well, greet, since she was supposed to be Julia, and Julia had probably met all these people, even though a huge number of them were from Julia's mother's company and Julia's father's hospital.

"You remember Doctor Biehl, don't you, Julia?" Julia's father asked.

"Of course," Maggie answered. The doctor kissed her cheek, and she tried not to wince as his bristly goatee brushed against her skin. "My father has been raving about your article on laser eye surgery," she said.

Dr. Biehl smiled. So did Julia's father.

I'm racking up some major brownie points for Julia, Maggie thought. *And I got her her boyfriend back.* But that last thought came with a twinge of guilt because Julia probably hadn't intended for Maggie to go kissing Tyler.

And that kiss. Maggie had never been kissed like that before. Even though she hated to admit it and had only admitted it to Scoz, she'd never been kissed for real. Wet, gross, obligation kisses during games of spin the bottle and truth or dare didn't count.

She'd been sure she was going to end up sweet sixteen and never kissed. And how pathetic would that be? But it turned out to be so not true. Her first real kiss was like something out of a movie—perfect. Absolutely perfect.

She shot a glance over at Tyler. He hadn't left her side since they'd entered the The Pierre's ballroom. He was great at the meet-and-greet stuff. Anytime Maggie faltered, Tyler was right there to pick up the slack.

He must have felt her eyes on him because he turned to face her. He leaned close. "About ten more minutes and I can hold you again," he whispered.

Maggie felt a flush spread over her entire body as her heart started up its want-that-want-that-now chant again. She managed to ignore it until she'd greeted every single person in the line. "You did a wonderful job, sweetheart," Julia's mother told Maggie. She moved Maggie's tiara a fraction of an inch to the left. "Your father has gone to tell the orchestra leader to start the spotlight dance. After that, you'll be free to have fun with your friends—as long as you don't ignore your other guests entirely."

Maggie nodded. Somehow she found Julia's mother much less annoying with Tyler standing next to her. It was as if the smell of him put her brain into some kind of trance or something. She could hardly form a thought beyond how badly she wanted to kiss him again.

"Looks like he's about to make the announcement," Tyler said, nodding toward the orchestra leader. Tyler smiled at Julia's mother, then took Maggie's hand and led her past the small round tables surrounding the huge dance floor. On each of the tables sat a flower bouquet surrounded by candles. The warmth of the candle flames seemed to make the flowers' aroma even stronger and sweeter. That, combined with the Tyler smell and the skin-to-skin contact of his hand on hers, was making Maggie almost dizzy, but in a good way.

"Ladies and gentlemen," the orchestra leader announced into his microphone. "Please join me in welcoming the birthday girl, Julia Reed-Prescott, who will be enjoying the first dance with her escort, Tyler Sanderson."

There was a burst of applause as Tyler led Maggie onto the floor and into the blazing spotlight. The sound faded—all sound faded—as Tyler took her into his arms. She didn't even know what song was playing. All she knew was Tyler's touch and the intensity in his eyes as he looked at her.

There were people gathered around the dance floor watching her, but she hardly saw them. The orchestra was a glimmering blur. All she saw was Tyler.

He's Julia's guy, a tiny voice in the back of Maggie's head reminded her. *Not tonight*, she answered it. Tonight was Maggie's Cinderella night, and Tyler was her prince. She was going to enjoy it, suck up every bit of it. That wouldn't hurt Julia. Tomorrow Julia would be the princess again. But tonight, just for tonight, all this was Maggie's.

Tyler spun Maggie around and lowered her into a deep dip. Slowly she became aware of the sound of applause again. The dance was over. It felt like it had only lasted an instant. An instant and an eternity at the same time.

"Your mother said we could hang with our friends now," Tyler said as he brought Maggie up from the dip. "I don't know about you, but what I need right now is to go out on the balcony for some *air*."

The way he emphasized the word *air* made it clear what he was really talking about.

"Air," Maggie repeated. "Yes." She fanned her face with her hand. "I need air."

She and Tyler wove their way through the couples flooding the dance floor. Without a moment's hesitation he found the door leading to the balcony. *I wonder if this is a familiar place to him,* Maggie thought. It was so grand and so special, it was hard to believe it could feel ordinary to anyone.

"Hurry," Tyler urged as he pulled back the thick brocade curtain and slid open the glass door. "If anyone sees us going out here, we'll have company."

Maggie definitely didn't want that. She rushed through the door, Tyler right behind her. And then— just the way it had happened in the limo—they were kissing. It was as if both their bodies were magnetized. Once they got close to each other—whompf—they had to make contact.

In an instant Tyler had Maggie pushed against the wall next to the door, his body flush against hers. It was as if he couldn't get close enough. Neither could Maggie. She met his soft lips with hers.

Together they entered another world, just as they had on the dance floor. It was a world they occupied alone, free of time, free of everything except the sensations of kissing and being kissed.

"I'm happy to see you two are getting along," a voice said, shattering their world. "But this is not appropriate. You both know better."

Maggie peered around Tyler's shoulder and saw Julia's mother studying them with cool eyes.

"You're right, Mrs. Prescott, I apologize," Tyler said, slipping right back into his party manner. He stepped away from Maggie and adjusted the collar on his tuxedo shirt.

"I'll go back in first," Tyler said. "It will be better than going out together." He cast a regretful glance at Maggie.

Julia's mother nodded. "Julia and I could use a moment alone."

Tyler scurried back inside the ballroom, and the balcony felt much chillier than it had before. Maggie wrapped her arms around herself. It didn't help.

"Is there anything you'd like to say about this spectacle?" Julia's mother asked in her low, well-bred voice.

"Spectacle?" Maggie burst out, her voice much higher than usual. "Why do you call it a spectacle? No one could see us. The curtain in front of the door was closed!"

"Let me rephrase," Julia's mother said. "Do you have

any explanation for rudely leaving your guests for so long? People were beginning to talk."

"And that's all you care about, isn't it?" Maggie demanded. "What people think. This whole party is about making a good impression on your and Dad's friends— not even your friends, your—your—" Maggie struggled to find the right word. "Your *colleagues*," she spit out.

"I will not be spoken to this way," Julia's mother said, her voice dropping even lower. "Your father and I went to great trouble and expense to give you this party—"

"And then you get mad when I try to have a little fun at *my* party," Maggie interrupted. "That's what parties are for—fun. Do you even know what that is?"

"First of all, I do not appreciate your language," Julia's mother hissed in a near whisper. "Second of all—" She gave a sharp shake of her head. "You are far too irrational for us to have this discussion right now. I'm going to return to the guests. Someone has to think about them." She turned on her heel and started to the door.

"Someone has to think of them because it would be bad for business not to!" Maggie snapped.

Julia's mother didn't turn around. "Go fix yourself up," she instructed. "It's almost time for cake." She opened the door and stepped through without a backward glance.

She's so sure I'll be a good girl and obey her orders, Maggie thought. Which she would. She didn't want to get Julia in more trouble than she already had—although she was glad she'd had the chance to point out that Julia's party had nothing to do with Julia.

Maggie gave a sigh. She stared at the open door for a moment. Then she pulled aside the fluttering curtain and headed back into the ballroom. It took her a few tries to find the ladies' room, but she finally got there. Each stall had its own sink and mirror, and Maggie stepped into the closest empty one to repair her makeup. Most of her lipstick had been kissed off.

"Could you believe Tyler?" a girl in one of the stalls asked.

Maggie's hand froze on the clasp of her tiny purse.

"What?" another girl asked.

"The way he was all lovey-dovey with Julia," the first girl said. Her voice sounded familiar, but Maggie wasn't sure why.

"Why wouldn't he be?" the other girl asked.

A toilet flushed, and Maggie heard the sound of a stall door opening. "Because," the first girl said, her voice closer now. "Yesterday I saw Elena and Tyler at

Drip, you know, the coffee shop, and she was all over him. I feel so bad for Julia."

"Shut up!" Maggie exploded. She burst out of the stall and wheeled around to face the girl. "You do not feel bad for me. You're enjoying yourself. Just the way you enjoyed telling me all about Elena's dress on the phone," Maggie continued, having placed where she'd first heard the girl's voice. This little pixie was Sydney Jane. Supposedly Julia's friend. *Yeah, right.*

"That's so unfair!" Sydney Jane exclaimed. "I told you because I care about you."

"You do not!" Maggie shot back. "Caring about me does not mean gossiping about me in the bathroom. It does not mean getting all excited about telling me bad news. And as for Tyler and Elena—Tyler and I got back together before the party. You can tell that to anyone you want."

Maggie slammed back into the stall and reapplied her lipstick with a steady hand. She smiled as she heard Sydney Jane flounce out of the bathroom. That had felt good. That had felt necessary. She didn't want anyone to walk around thinking they could treat Julia like dirt. She hoped Miss Big Mouth would pass the news along—Julia was no longer to be messed with.

"Julia, if it means anything, I think you're right,"

called the girl Sydney Jane had been spreading her nasty gossip to. She was still in the next stall over. "Sydney Jane pretends like she's upset when things go wrong for people. But she really loves it. She's like a pain vampire or something."

"Thank you, whoever you are," Maggie called to the voice.

"It's Amanda," the girl answered.

"Thank you, Amanda," Maggie said. She reminded herself to tell JuJu that Amanda was a girl who might actually be worth her time.

"See you back out there," Amanda said.

Maggie put on a little more eye shadow. She wasn't usually much of a makeup person, but you couldn't wear a tiara without makeup. It was just wrong.

"Now go blow out your candles like a good girl," she whispered to her reflection. "Then you can get yourself some more Tyler time." *When Julia gets him back, he's not going to even remember the name Elena,* she promised herself.

The thought of giving Tyler back hurt more than Maggie wanted to think about right now. She pushed away the pain. She'd deal with all of it tomorrow when she was back in the real world.

Maggie squared her shoulders, lifted her chin, and

made her way back into the ballroom. She was stopped again and again for more mindless, polite chat, but eventually she reached the table at the front of the room. On it sat an enormous white birthday cake, gleaming with candles and surrounded by flowers. A moment later Julia's parents were at her side. At a signal from Julia's father the orchestra paused and then broke into the familiar opening of "Happy Birthday." Everyone gathered around to sing.

Maggie watched and listened with big party smiles as flashbulbs popped. She felt as glamorous as any celebrity in her shimmering dress, her face aglow in the light of the candles. She made a big show of blowing out all sixteen candles, and everybody clapped wildly. Her princess night wouldn't last forever, and she wanted to make the most of it.

"Thank you all so much for coming," Maggie called as the crowd quieted. "You've all helped make this the most special birthday of my life." She scanned the faces for the person who really had made it her best birthday ever, but she didn't see Tyler anywhere.

Maggie was about to go look for him, but Julia's father snagged her for a dance, which was actually pretty sweet of him. Then Julia's mother insisted she go over to the Sandersons' table. She hoped Tyler would be with them, but he wasn't.

After what felt like an endless conversation: "What a beautiful dress!" "Isn't the orchestra wonderful!" "This cake is delicious!" Julia made her escape. The ballroom was huge, but after a couple of laps around it, Maggie was convinced that Tyler wasn't inside.

"Where did he go?" she muttered. "He has to know that I'd be looking for him." A grin spread across her face. Of course Tyler knew she'd be looking for him. So he went back to *their* place. The balcony.

Maggie hurried over as fast as her high heels would take her. She pulled open the brocade curtain. Tyler was there!

Her heart slammed into her stomach, then ricocheted into her throat.

Yes, Tyler was there—and he was kissing another girl. A girl in a dress cut down to her butt.

Julia's Birthday Presents

3 MP3 players
2 mini disc players
1 laser disc player
2 Kate Spade backpacks
100 savings bonds
33 pieces of assorted jewelry from Tiffany's
350 assorted CDs
55 assorted laser discs
1 personal digital assistant
7 fountain pens from Tiffany's
11 silver picture frames from Tiffany's
1 iMac
4 StarTAC cell phones
2 pairs of Armani sunglasses
4 tickets to the revival of *Long Day's Journey into Night*
1 round-trip ticket to France *(for trip with maternal grandparents)*
1 round-trip ticket to Africa *(for trip with paternal grandparents)*
1 Volvo

Julia forced a smile at the girl sitting across from her at one of the long tables in the church basement. Rachel, she reminded herself. Her name is Rachel. Rachel, Rachel, Rachel.

"This lasagna is fantastic," Julia told Rachel.

"Um-huh," Rachel mumbled, her mouth full.

Julia took a bite of her roll. Her stomach was still feeling a little queasy, and bread seemed like the safest choice. "The bread is really good, too," she added.

The bread is really good, too, she repeated silently. *I sound like a total idiot. Or the world's most boring person.*

Which maybe she was. Yes, Julia knew how to handle herself in social situations. She knew how to make chitchat—and usually she came up with something slightly better than "the bread is really good, too." She knew how to sit, how to stand, how to walk, how to eat, how to make an introduction. But it was possible—very possible—to know all those things and still be the most boring person in the history of boredom.

Julia scanned the basement, hoping for inspiration. She'd already commented on the seventies disco decorations. Her eyes lit on Scoz, who was making his way back to their table with what looked like a second helping of everything from the buffet. Julia smiled, a real, not-just-being-polite smile, as he hurried over and sat back down beside her.

"Okay, time for the desert island game," he announced to the group around the table. "Who would you rather be trapped on a desert island with? Batman or Superman?"

"Batman, definitely," the girl next to Rachel—Dax, her name was—answered. "He's way sexier."

"Yeah, Batman," Rachel agreed. "What about you, Mike?" she asked.

Mike, Julia repeated to herself, relieved to have figured out another name. And extremely relieved that Scoz had taken control of the table's conversation.

"Are we taking away Superman's ability to fly?" Mike asked, running his fingers over one of his sideburns. "Because if we aren't, then there's really absolutely no reason for either of us to be on the island. If, however, Superman is un—"

"Next!" Scoz interrupted.

"Buffy the Vampire Slayer," the short guy at the head

of the table—Julia was still waiting for someone to use his name—jumped in.

Instantly he was pelted with food from every side. "The choices are Batman and Superman!" Rachel yelled. "You can't say Buffy when the choices are Batman and Superman. You can't—"

"I think we got the point," Scoz cut in.

"*We* might have the point, but *he* doesn't," Rachel continued, an edge of hysteria in her voice. "He always says Buffy. He's obsessed with Buffy. He—"

The Buffy guy silenced her by leaning over and kissing her. It was a long kiss that sent a blush to Julia's face. "I've always thought you looked a little like Buffy," he said as he pulled away.

Everyone laughed, including Julia.

"Okay, Mags, you're up," Scoz said.

Julia had a horrifying vision of herself explaining that she would choose Superman because the bread was really good, except Batman might make a better choice because the lasagna was fantastic.

"No thinking! Just answer!" Scoz told her.

"Superman," Julia blurted out.

A piece of bread bounced off her forehead. "Superman is a dork!" Dax called. "Why would you possibly choose Superman?"

Julia used her napkin to wipe away the little smear of butter left by the bread missile and considered the question. "Think about it," she told Dax. "You're on a desert island. You'd want someone to talk to, right? Someone for company? But Batman is so moody. He'd be off in a cave somewhere. At least Superman is polite. He'd make conversation."

"Good answer," Scoz said, game-show-host style. "Now—"

"What is that hideous sound?" The Buffy guy groaned, looking around the room.

Julia listened. "It's 'You Are So Beautiful to Me,'" she answered.

"Somebody make it stop!" Mike cried, his palms clamped over his ears.

Julia felt a hand on her shoulder. She glanced back and saw Maggie's dad standing there. "Will you dance with me?" he asked.

"You *requested* this song, didn't you? You actually went up to the DJ and—" the Buffy guy accused.

Julia and Maggie's father both ignored him. Julia smiled at him and stood, and Maggie's father took her hand. He led her out into the section of the basement that had been cleared for dancing. There was a group *awww* as he pulled her into his arms.

144

"So are you going to be able to forgive me?" Maggie's father asked, his voice husky.

"It might take some time . . . but yes," Julia answered. She thought that was true. No matter how furious Maggie was, she wouldn't be able to hate her father for the rest of her life. They were much too close for that.

"Fair enough," Maggie's father answered. Julia was relieved that he hadn't decided to try and make her talk out the situation. That was something he should do with the real Maggie.

They danced in silence for a moment. Then Julia made herself ask the question she didn't really want answered. "Is *she* here? You know."

Maggie's father shook his head. "Not yet. She probably wanted to give you some time with your friends before she showed up." He guided her into a twirl under his arm, then pulled her close enough to sing into her ear, "You're all I've ever hoped for. Da dum da dum da dee. You are so beautiful to me."

Julia blinked to clear away the layer of tears coating her eyes. *I wonder if my dad danced with me at my party?* she thought as the song came to an end, a tendril of longing wrapping around her heart.

Maggie's father held her a moment longer, then gave

her hand a squeeze and released her. "If you want me with you when you talk to Ann—to your mother, I'll be there," he promised.

Julia nodded and started back toward her table. "Not so fast!" a voice boomed. She jerked her head toward the sound and saw that Mike had abducted the DJ's microphone. He gave her a wicked grin. "There's been a request for your famously shagadelic go-go dance."

This isn't happening, Julia thought. *This cannot be happening.*

The lights in the basement dimmed, then the mirror ball overhead began to spin, sending sparkles around the room. A pink strobe light started to pulse in time to the pounding sixties music. A moment later a green strobe was added to the mix.

Julia's entire body felt frozen. She stood there, motionless, a deer in the strobe lights.

A rhythmic clapping started up. Then a chant—"Mag-gie. Mag-gie. Mag-gie."

They weren't going to let her get out of this. What was she going to do? Years of ballet lessons and Miss Godwin's ridiculous white-glove tea dances weren't going to help her out. "Mag-gie! Mag-gie! Mag-gie!" The cheers were borderline hysterical now.

Hot bile rose in Julia's throat. *Oh, no. Please, God, no,*

she thought. She couldn't throw up here in front of everyone. At Coney Island, in front of strangers, it was humiliating enough, even though Scoz had—

Scoz. She needed Scoz. She scanned the room, found him, locked her eyes on him. Her brain flickered back to life, and an idea filled her head.

Maggie approached Scoz. She turned her back and shimmied her way down the length of him. She felt like a huge idiot, but she got some whoops of encouragement, so she grooved away from Scoz, then shot him a seductive glance over her shoulder and beckoned to him. Instantly he followed her. He pursed his lips and raised his eyebrows at her in a hugely exaggerated come-on.

Julia laughed. She batted her eyes and gave him another shimmy. She wasn't sure what she was doing, but at least she was doing *something,* and it felt good.

Rachel and the Buffy guy came over to them and started dancing. Mike and Dax joined the group a second later. Now Julia had four people to watch and imitate. But she didn't bother. She just listened to the music and did *whatever.*

It was like being back in the front car of the roller coaster again. Julia was falling, flying. She let out a little shout of pure joy. Then she pulled Scoz toward her and bumped his hip with hers. He bumped her hip right back. Hips swaying, they bumped back and forth, lowering their bodies closer and closer to the ground while their friends circled them, clapping and shouting. Julia's legs were shaking with the exertion. Laughing, she missed Scoz's hip and grabbed his shoulders for balance. He tried to steady her but lost his balance, too, and they both landed in a tangle on the floor. Everybody was laughing and screaming as the song ended.

For an instant, lying there on the floor, they stared at each other. Julia's gaze flicked from Scoz's eyes, green as new leaves, to his lips, perfectly shaped under the black lipstick. She had a wild impulse to kiss him, but she scrambled to her feet before she could give in to it, reminding herself that Scoz and Maggie were just friends.

"Time for the presents," Rachel called. She grabbed Julia by the arm and pulled her back over to their table. By the time she sat down, there was a heap of presents in front of her.

Julia reached for the closest one and hesitated. She felt eyes on her.

Of course you do, she told herself. *Everyone is looking at you right now because they want to see what you got.* She carefully untied the glittery ribbon, a prickly sensation running from the top of her neck to the base of her spine.

Julia glanced behind her. All the way in the back of the group stood a woman. There was no question that she was Maggie's mother. The resemblance between her and Maggie—and Julia—was amazing. Maggie's mother gave Julia a small, tentative smile. Julia smiled back, her lips trembling slightly.

"Just rip it open," Dax exclaimed impatiently.

Julia turned back around and, following instructions, tore open the gift. She opened present after present, making the appropriate ooohs and aaahs, on complete autopilot. Her mind was fully occupied by what she could possibly say to Maggie's mother.

When the last gift was finally open, she leaned over to Scoz. "She's here. My mother. I'm going to go talk to her."

Scoz grabbed her hand and gave it a hard squeeze. "Want me to come?" he asked.

Julia shook her head. She stood up. "Thanks so much, everyone," she called out. Then she made her way without hesitation to Maggie's mother. She was afraid if she allowed herself to hesitate, she'd end up running in the opposite direction, and that wasn't exactly what her deal with Maggie had been. Julia had promised to make chitchat, and that's what she was going to do.

Julia didn't look up until she was standing directly in front of the woman. Maggie's mother looked at least as nervous as Julia felt. "I'm . . ." The woman's words trailed off, and she angled her gaze away from Julia.

"I know," Julia answered.

"D-do you think maybe we could go upstairs for a minute?" Maggie's mother asked, still not able to look at Julia.

"Okay," Julia said, although it would have been much easier to keep things light and impersonal if they were surrounded by other people.

Maggie's mother led the way over to the narrow wooden staircase and up to the first floor. She paused for a moment, then turned right and headed into the sanctuary. They slid into the back pew, and a velvety silence enveloped them.

Julia stared at the candles to the left of the altar as she waited for Maggie's mother to speak. Julia hadn't been raised Catholic, but she knew that each of the candles had been lit for a reason, by a person with a prayer. Had Maggie's mother lit one before she came down to the party? Julia shoved the thought away.

As she watched, one of the candle flames flickered

150

and went out. *It's like a sign*, she thought. *A sign that I should be gentle with Maggie's mother.*

Julia tried to push that thought away, too. She wasn't here to bring about a reconciliation between Maggie and her mother. She was here to keep Maggie from having to deal with her mother even one time. She had to remember that.

"I rehearsed what I was going to say so many times," Maggie's mother admitted in a rush. "But now I've forgotten all of it."

Julia glanced at her. Maggie's mother's eyes were focused on the candles Julia had been staring at. Had she seen one of the flames go out, too?

"You don't need a speech," Julia said.

"I shouldn't need a speech to talk to my own daughter," Maggie's mother answered, eyes still on the candles. "But you're not just my daughter—you're a stranger, too. I keep thinking how much you must hate me."

Julia didn't answer. There was nothing she could say to comfort Maggie's mother that wouldn't betray Maggie.

"I would hate me if I were you. I hated my own mother for leaving me, and she left by dying." Maggie's mother gave a harsh bark of laughter. Then she turned to face Julia, and Julia could see the shimmer of tears in her eyes.

"I don't have nearly such a good reason for leaving you," Maggie's mother said. She reached out as if to touch Julia's arm, but then gripped the top of the pew instead. "When I got pregnant . . . I felt as if every decision for the rest of my life had been made for me. I could see what every day would be, every day, at least from sixteen to thirty-six or so. Which felt like my whole entire life."

Julia nodded. She completely understood. She felt like her whole life had been planned, too. The right college, then married to the right guy, probably Tyler. Plus the right job, maybe at her mother's company or perhaps at her father's hospital. A small apartment. Then a bigger apartment. Kids. No surprises. No choices.

"It's not even that the days looked bad," Maggie's mother continued. "I loved your father, and although I'm sure it's impossible to believe, I knew I would love you." Her grip on the pew tightened. "I did love you. Do love you." Her voice broke with emotion.

"I know," Julia answered. She couldn't help herself. "Dad gave me your cards and letters today. It was the first time I'd seen them."

Maggie's mother gave a sound that was part sigh and

part whimper. "I wasn't sure if he'd give them to you at all," she admitted.

"Then why didn't you ever call me?" Julia burst out, feeling an unexpected flare of anger on Maggie's behalf. "You could have tried. Or you could have come. I know you live in California, but you could have come before now."

One tear escaped and rolled down the woman's cheek. "For a bunch of years I wasn't the kind of person I would want my daughter to associate with. Then I . . . got it together, but . . ." She viciously wiped the tear away. "But it felt too late. How could I just show up after all I had missed?"

"But you did," Julia said softly.

"Because I started thinking about you. No, not started," Maggie's mother corrected herself. "I always thought about you, even when I was spending all my energy doing things so I wouldn't think about you. More recently I started worrying about you. Worrying that you might make some of the mistakes I had. And I started to think maybe something good—for both of us—could happen if I tried to see you."

She turned and touched Julia's cheek, very quickly, with trembling fingers. "I just had to know that you were okay."

"I am," Julia answered. "Dad is completely there for me. And I have good friends. I'm fine." She knew Maggie's mother was hoping for something else, something more, some indication that maybe someday she could have a place in Maggie's life.

But there was nothing else Julia could say, not even when the tears began to fall down Maggie's mother's face again, not even when tears began to sting Julia's own eyes.

"Thank you for talking to me," Maggie's mother mumbled. Then she scrambled up from the pew and rushed out of the sanctuary.

Julia dropped her chin to her chest, letting the tears fall. She pulled in a few deep breaths, then pushed herself to her feet, stepped out of the pew, and turned to the door. Then she changed directions and walked up to the altar.

It took her only a moment to find the candle that had gone out. When she did, she relit it, adding a prayer of her own, a prayer for Maggie and her mother to find . . . peace.

Maggie's birthday presents

1 collection of Pez dispensers, with Pez
10 assorted CDs
1 onyx ring that once belonged to Maggie's paternal great-great-great-grandmother
1 leather-bound diary
2 Teletubbies gone goth
1 box Jelly Belly jelly beans—forty flavors
1 soccer ball with the face of Maggie's history teacher drawn on in Magic Marker
1 mood ring
1 silver heart necklace
1 hamburger made out of soap
1 book (*The Complete Idiot's Guide to Investing*)
6 assorted videotapes
1 Body Shop gift basket
2 dragonfly barrettes
1 certificate for a pool lesson
1 photo album

Maggie blinked back the tears of hurt and anger that were turning the figures on the balcony into blurry blotches of color. As quietly as she could, she slid the glass door open a few inches.

It wouldn't have mattered if I'd set off an atomic bomb, she thought. Elena—the girl had to be the famous Elena—and Tyler would have kept groping each other until their bodies melted into radioactive goop.

As Maggie stood there, watching them, she could almost feel Tyler's lips on hers. Her skin still ached for him, even though her brain knew with complete certainty that he was the lowest form of scum. She could almost understand why Julia had wanted him back even after he'd treated her so badly. Tyler was like a drug or something.

And it was time to kick the habit. Kick it to the curb.

"I've got to go back in and find Julia. I promised my parents I'd be a good boy tonight," Maggie heard Tyler say, even though his face was buried in Elena's long hair.

chapter

12

"I'm not letting you go," Elena answered. She turned her head slightly, and Maggie realized she was the cow who'd been so snotty to Maggie at the spa that afternoon.

They deserve each other, Maggie thought. But that didn't mean she was going to let them waltz off into the sunset together. She was getting revenge—for herself and for JuJu. She just had to figure out how.

"I've really got to get out there," Tyler insisted. "But don't worry. You have an appointment with Doctor Love in the backseat of the limo as soon as I drop Julia off tonight."

He pulled himself away from Elena, and Maggie let the curtain fall back in place over the door. She turned and walked quickly away. She needed a place to think, to plan. Without quite deciding to go there, she ended up back in the ladies' room. She hit the door at the same moment as a sophisticated-looking red-haired girl.

"We have to stop meeting like this," the girl joked.

Maggie recognized the voice—this had to be Amanda, the cool chick who'd agreed that Sydney Jane was a gossip monster. "Hey, are you all right?" Amanda asked as they stepped inside.

"Actually, no," Maggie admitted.

Amanda held up one finger. "Wait," she said. She made a pass through the bathroom, checking under each stall door. "Okay, we're alone. Spill it."

Maggie didn't have the feeling that Amanda and Julia were incredibly close. But Maggie's gut said she could trust Amanda, and even though it was the same gut that said she should believe Tyler's bull, Maggie decided to go with it.

"I just saw Tyler and Elena giving each other physicals out on the balcony. Sydney Jane was right about the two of them," Maggie admitted. "I'm so annoyed at myself. At him, too. But mostly at me. I knew he was a player—so completely knew it—and then I let him play me."

"Welcome to the club," Amanda answered. "Actually, I've been wanting to talk to you about Tyler for a while. But the way you looked at him, all glowing, I just couldn't do it."

Maggie sat down on the padded velvet bench. "Don't tell me. He played you, too."

Amanda sat down beside her and picked at one of the bench's covered buttons. "Big time. During Christmas break he started sniffing around me. Told me that he'd broken up with you. Since we weren't in school where I could see the two of you together, I believed him. It took him about three days to convince me that I was totally in love with him."

"Three days," Maggie repeated. "It didn't even take him three hours to get me back tonight. He got all sincere and told me that he'd only broken up with me because he was so sick of his parents pushing him to be with me. Then he fed me this load of garbage about the two of us being soul mates. He was like, 'Baby, can't you feel our souls twining around each other? They want to be together.'"

Amanda looked slightly nauseated. "You know where he got that don't you?" she asked. She grabbed Maggie's arm and squeezed hard. "From me. You wouldn't believe the e-mails I sent him. It makes me sick to think about it. They were so pathetically mushy."

"That soul mate stuff was from you?" Maggie cried.

"Much as I hate to admit it—yeah," Amanda answered, taking back her hand. She started twisting the velvet-covered button again.

Maggie was silent for a few seconds. "You know what? I think I just came up with a way to end Tyler's days as a player," Maggie told her. "Are you in?"

"There is nothing I'd rather do," Amanda answered, her blue eyes gleaming. She gave the button such a hard twist that it popped free.

"First, we need to find a computer," Maggie said. Her blood was starting to feel electrified.

Amanda sprang to her feet. "I bet there's one in the manager's office. And with the amount your parents had to have paid for this party—"

"I'm sure he'll be happy to let us use it," Maggie finished for her. "Come on." She rushed out of the bathroom, snagged the closest waiter, and got directions to the manager's office, then she and Amanda headed straight there.

As soon as the guy found out that Maggie was the birthday girl, he was happy to take a break and let her and Amanda use his computer in private.

"Okay, here's the tricky part," Maggie said. She clicked on the AOL icon. "I want to retrieve some of Tyler's e-mail. I know his screen name, but we're going to have to guess his password."

She signed on as a guest, using the name T-man3.

"So we've got to think like Tyler," Amanda answered. She shoved some of the manager's paperwork out of the way and sat down on the desk next to the computer. "We know he's not very creative. Try *sexgod.*"

Maggie typed in the password. A message came back a moment later, saying it was invalid. She tried the word *player.* Invalid. *Numberone.* Invalid.

"We've got to figure this out!" Maggie cried, the electric feeling in her blood intensifying by a couple of amps. "It's got to happen tonight. Now. I don't want to leave this party until Tyler is down for the count."

"Oh, I know, I know!" Amanda exclaimed. "Doctor Love! He used to call himself that all the time."

Maggie's eyes widened. "I just heard him call himself that to Elena out on the balcony. That's it. It's got to be." She typed in *drlove,* her fingers slamming down on the keys. A moment later a computerized voice said, "Welcome. You've got mail."

"Oh my God!" Maggie and Amanda screamed at the same time. They slapped hands victoriously. "Now we get to see what our little Tyler's been up to," Maggie said. She hit the icon of the mailbox with the flag up, then selected the "mail-you've-sent" file. Tyler had sent six messages that were tagged "Re: Soul Mates." Each of the six messages was to a different girl. Maggie printed them all out.

Then she printed out five copies of the "Re: Green, green grass" e-mail. Each was identical to the "Re: Green, green grass" e-mail he'd sent to Julia. Each was to a different girl.

Maggie also found seven copies of the "Re: You" e-mail. Of course, the "Re: You" messages were all slightly different. Instead of a string of "Juliajuliajuliajulia" there was "Jessicajessicajessica" and "Elenaelenaelenaelena." And so on. "He is so busted," Maggie muttered.

"He just took my e-mails to him and recycled them. What an incredible slimebucket," Amanda said. "He didn't even bother to retype anything but the names. It's one big cut-and-paste job."

"Do you have your originals?" Maggie asked. "Then we could show that not only is Tyler a scumbag; he's so lame, he can't even write his own mail."

"Log off, and then I'll log on as me and get them," Amanda said. "I kept saving them just to torture myself. And to remind myself never to get suckered like that again."

Maggie hit the button to exit AOL and moved aside. Amanda accessed her account a minute later. She printed out the e-mails she'd sent to Tyler. "I feel like such a fool," she admitted as she gathered up the sheets of paper.

"You're in good company," Maggie answered. She waved the sheaf of e-mails Tyler had sent out.

"So now what?" Amanda asked.

Maggie smiled mischievously. "Did you notice that the wallpaper in the ladies' room is a little *dingy?*" Maggie asked. She turned around and stuck the printouts of the e-mail in the hotel manager's copy machine.

Amanda grinned as she leaned across Maggie, added her printouts to the stack, selected fifteen copies, and pressed start. "Very dingy," she agreed.

When the copies were finished, Maggie grabbed them and a roll of tape, then she and Amanda returned to the ladies' room. It didn't take long for them to plaster the place with Tyler's love notes to all his assorted girls, along with the source material.

"Suddenly I'm in the mood for something gooey and chocolaty," Amanda said as she surveyed their work. "To celebrate."

"I'm with you," Maggie agreed. "There's just one thing I've got to do first."

Maggie hurried back out into the party and wandered through the ballroom, searching, searching, searching. At last she found the person she was looking for.

"Hello, Elena," Maggie said in the silky-snotty voice she'd been perfecting all day. "I hope you're having an enjoyable time."

"Very," Elena answered with a smirk.

Maggie allowed a tiny frown to appear on her face. "Your lipstick is a little smeared," she commented. "You might want to stop by the ladies' room."

WHAT I THOUGHT OF TYLER

at 8:00 p.m.
1. Hot
2. Hot
3. Hot
4. Hot
5. Hot
6. Hot
7. Hot
8. Hot
9. Hot
10. 100% Hot

at 10:00 p.m.
1. Scum
2. Scum
3. Scum
4. Scum
5. Scum
6. Scum
7. Scum
8. Scum
9. Scum
10. 100% Scum

The tears in Julia's eyes turned the cars along Seventh Avenue into streaks of light—red taillights and white headlights. She wrapped her arms around herself and huddled on one end of the bus stop bench. She couldn't go back into the party yet. Maggie's mother was there, and Julia needed some more time to regain her composure.

She could have stayed in the sanctuary, but looking at all those flickering candles, all those prayers, made her feel sad. Probably because she knew how one of those prayers had been answered tonight.

chapter 13

Julia sighed, unable to shake the feeling that somehow she could have handled the conversation with Maggie's mother better, although right now she had no idea how.

"Waiting for your driver?" a familiar voice asked. A moment later Scoz sat down next to her.

"I'm afraid he got jacked," Julia answered with a small smile. It seemed forever ago that she and Scoz had had this conversation the first time. So much had happened since then; some of it wonderful, some of it heartbreaking.

"So, come on, talk. How did it go with your mother?" Scoz asked.

The sympathy in his voice was too much for Julia. She couldn't stop the tears from spilling down her cheeks. "It was so hard," she burst out. "And so confusing."

Scoz reached out and wiped away her tears with his fingers. "Sorry. I had to throw away my bandanna because it had puke all over it," he reminded her.

Julia gave a choked laugh.

"So how did you two leave it?" Scoz asked. "Or should I just shut up and not ask any more questions?"

"No, it's okay, really" Julia answered. She needed someone to talk to, and Scoz was the perfect person, although she never would have believed that ten hours ago.

I'm going to miss him, she realized, a fresh ache starting in the spot under her ribs. She wished there was some way they could stay friends. But if he found out the truth about her, he'd have no interest in seeing her again. What would Little Miss Boring have to interest a guy like Scoz?

Julia knew he'd be nice about it because that was just

the kind of guy he was. But that's all he would be doing—being nice.

She pushed the thoughts out of her mind and turned her attention back to the situation between Maggie and her mother. When Maggie and Julia switched back lives, Maggie would probably want to talk to Scoz about her mother. It would be good if he knew the whole story. Maybe he'd be able to help Maggie understand a little.

"It would be easier if I could hate her," Julia told Scoz. "If I could just say that what she did was completely unforgivable."

"But?" Scoz said. He pulled off his leather vest and wrapped it around her shoulders. "You have to be freezing in that excuse for a dress."

Julia pulled the vest tighter around her. The leather was still warm from Scoz's skin, and she found that comforting in some way that went deeper than its warmth.

"But she told me that when she got pregnant, she felt like every moment for almost the rest of her life had been decided," Julia explained. "She was only sixteen when I was born. Only my age. And I know how bad that feels. It's like being in a cage when all your choices have been made for you. It's not that I'm saying what she did was right or even that I would have done the

169

same thing she did, but I understand. Sometimes in the cage you feel like you're going crazy."

"What's your cage?" Scoz asked, his green eyes intent as he waited for her answer.

"My cage is where I'll go to school, and where I'll live, and where I'll work, and who I'll marry. It's all been decided for me. I get to decide if I'll wear the lavender twinset or the cream one, but other than that—" Julia stopped short, horrified to realize she'd answered as herself and not Maggie.

Scoz stared at her for at least a minute. "Are you going to tell me who you really are?" he asked, his tone mild. "Because unless you've recently developed a brain tumor, you are not now, nor have you been for at least the last bunch of hours, Maggie Watkins."

"You knew all along?" Julia asked, her voice coming out in a squeak.

"I knew something was very weird—starting with you offering me a snack. Maggie would never do that," Scoz answered. "But I admit, I didn't actually think that the weirdness came from Maggie not even being Maggie. That's pretty tough to imagine."

Julia nodded. "Maggie and I met each other at the DMV this morning. We couldn't believe it when we saw each other. And then we discovered it was both our

Sweet Sixteens. We were both dreading our parties. So we decided to switch just for tonight," Julia explained in a rush.

"*The Prince and the Pauper*," Scoz muttered.

"Yeah. It's like *The Prince and the Pauper*," Julia agreed. Suddenly she felt like she'd been sucking in helium instead of oxygen. Her whole body felt light with the relief of having told the truth.

"I know why Maggie was dreading tonight. But what about you?" Scoz asked.

Julia shook her head. It seemed kind of silly now. She could hardly pull up a picture of Tyler's face, let alone the hurt feelings that had been so strong this morning. "My ex-boyfriend was coming to my party with another girl, probably the most beautiful girl in school."

"Ouch," Scoz said.

"Ouch," Julia agreed. "Although I shouldn't have cared so much. He treated me like dirt. I should have been happy to be rid of him."

"It doesn't usually work that way, though," Scoz answered.

The change in his tone made Julia realize he was talking from personal experience. "Lainie?" she asked.

"How do you even know about that?" he asked.

"Maggie let me read her diary," Julia admitted. "I

only skimmed. I was trying to figure out your name." She smiled. "You do not want to know what was going through my head when you came up to me outside the Burger Castle."

"Yes, I do," Scoz insisted.

Julia giggled, the helium relief making her light-headed. "No, no, no."

Scoz studied her for a minute. "You really do look exactly like Maggie," he said. "I wonder if that means that you have the same tickle spot as she does."

Before Julia could completely register what he'd said, Scoz's fingers were on her sides, tickling her mercilessly. "Tell me," he insisted.

Julia tried to twist away, but Scoz was too fast.

"I thought you were a freak!" she burst out. "You scared me to death. But now—"

Scoz stopped tickling. "But now," he repeated.

Julia tried to catch her breath. "Now I think you're the sweetest, most wonderful guy I have ever met," she admitted. And she did something she'd never done before. She took the initiative, leaned forward, and kissed Scoz lightly on the lips.

She pulled away fast, her cheeks burning. What had she done? What total humiliation. Now Scoz was going to have to be nice to her. Now he was going to have to try not to hurt her feelings and come up with some polite reason why he—

"What?" Scoz asked. "What's wrong?"

"Nothing," Julia answered, unable to meet his eyes.

He reached over and ran his thumb across her bottom lip. "You got a little of my lipstick on you," he said. He shook his head. "I haven't kissed anyone since I went to the goth side. I hadn't thought about that part of it."

"It's okay," Julia said.

"But something's wrong," Scoz insisted. "Maggie can never fool me, and neither can you. Am I going to have to tickle you again?"

"It's just . . . you have no idea who I really am," Julia answered. "If you did . . ." She couldn't complete the thought.

"Are you an escaped convict?" Scoz asked with mock eagerness. "Because there is something very sexy about that. If they capture you, I swear I'll write every day."

"All I am is a prep school girl," Julia said.

Scoz recoiled. "You go to prep school?" he cried, one hand pressed to his chest.

"Yes," Julia replied. "And my parents have a ton of money. And I wear twinsets."

"I don't know if I can take any more," Scoz exclaimed.

But then he looked at her, and his face grew serious. "Why is this a problem?"

"Because you're never going to want to see me again. I'm way too boring. And—and—my parents and their friends are really uptight," she admitted, shocked that she was actually telling him the truth. "And if I don't ever get to see you again, I—" She forced herself to stop. She'd said too much already.

"What is your name, anyway?" Scoz asked.

Julia pulled in a shaky breath. "Julia Reed-Prescott," she answered.

Scoz studied her for a moment. "And Julia Reed-Prescott, at this prep school you go to, do you have to wear those little plaid skirts? Because second only to my women-behind-bars obsession is my thing for those skirts."

"You don't have to try to make me feel better," Julia told him. "It's okay."

"I'm not trying to make you feel better," Scoz exploded. "You act like you just told me something hideous about yourself. I'm trying to make you see what an idiot you are. So what if you go to prep school? That doesn't make you . . . anything. Except someone who goes to prep school."

Julia rubbed the back of her neck with her fingers. "You're right. That isn't fair. Not everyone who goes to prep school is boring."

"Would you stop with this boring crap!" Scoz shouted. "You're not boring. I saw you on the roller coaster. You were into it with every molecule. When you get that . . . that *involved,* you can't be boring."

Julia started to reply, but Scoz kept going.

"I saw you on the dance floor tonight, too. That dance, the way you looked at me, the way you moved— whoa. Definitely not boring. And that kiss—" He grinned at her. "Okay, the kiss was a little boring, but nice."

"Boring?" Julia repeated. But her body felt so light now that she was surprised she hadn't floated away. She cupped Scoz's face in her hands and kissed him again, trying to express everything she was feeling with her lips.

Scoz gave a muffled groan and slid Julia into his lap. Julia thought she heard a bus pull up and people get out. Vaguely she was aware that she was making a spectacle of herself . . . again.

But she didn't care. All she cared about was the sensations of Scoz's hands on her waist, his lips on hers.

Julia pulled back just a fraction. "Boring?" she mumbled against Scoz's lips.

"No way," he answered, his lips brushing against hers. "Absolutely fascinating."

WHAT I THOUGHT OF SCOZ

When I first met him: After our first kiss:

1. Scary
2. Freaky
3. Creepy
4. Dangerous
5. Weird
6. Threatening
7. Strange
8. Abnormal
9. Deviant
10. Something to avoid

1. Sweet
2. Adorable
3. Funny
4. Empathetic
5. Sexy
6. Good
7. Playful
8. Loyal
9. Smart
10. Mine

Maggie stepped out of the Pierre hotel, happy to leave Julia's Sweet Sixteen party behind her. Although it had been fun seeing Tyler get slapped twice—once by Elena and once by a girl Maggie hadn't met, who had also been on the receiving end of one of his e-mail love bombs.

Maybe I should have given him a couple of slaps myself, she thought. *One good one for me. And one good one for Julia.*

No, she decided. It was more satisfying knowing that she had arranged for the truth about Tyler to come out. A slap only lasted for a second, but Maggie suspected Tyler was going to have a very hard time getting a new girlfriend, at least a new girlfriend in his *social circle,* for a long, long, long time.

chapter 14

She couldn't wait to describe both of the slaps to Julia. "She should be here by now. We said we'd trade back at eleven," Maggie muttered. She peered down the street. She spotted a homeless woman gathering cans and bottles out of the trash, but other than that, the block was empty.

Maggie shifted impatiently from foot to foot. Her anxiety about what had gone down between Julia and her mother doubled with every second. She'd been trying not to think about it all night, but now there were no distractions, and thoughts of her mother attacked every section of her brain.

"Maggie!" a voice cried out.

Maggie whipped her head toward the sound and saw Julia rushing down the block toward her—hand in hand with Scoz! *What happened here?* she wondered as she flew down the street toward them.

She and Julia hugged each other and started talking at the same instant.

"Hold on," Scoz called. "One of you has to go first."

"You," Maggie ordered, pointing at Julia. "Start with that." She lowered her finger to Julia and Scoz's joined hands.

"He knows what's really going on," Julia admitted. "I wasn't all that wonderful at pretending to be you. And, um, he likes me." She gave a goofy grin.

"You should have seen her on the Cyclone," Scoz cut in. "I've lost at least twenty-five percent hearing ability in each ear. That's how loud she was screaming."

"You could have told me your best friend was a goth guy," Julia added. "At first I had to picture him with a pocket protector and really thick glasses just to stay in the same room with him."

Scoz gave a growl and swooped Julia up in the air. He spun her around in a circle. "You were right to be scared. Just wait until I get you alone." Julia giggled frantically, having trouble stopping even when Scoz put her down.

"You didn't by any chance run into a *third* identical stranger tonight and make another switch, did you?" Maggie asked, shaking her head. "Because you do not seem like the same girl who was sniveling in the DMV bathroom this morning."

"I don't feel like that girl, either," Julia admitted.

Maggie felt a jab of envy at how happy Julia sounded. She'd clearly had a much better night than Maggie had. And Scoz looked happier than he had in months. It looked like he might have actually found an antidote for Lainie that didn't involve punching more holes in his hide.

"I guess you want to know how it went with—," Julia began, suddenly turning serious.

"First you have to hear what I did to Tyler," Maggie interrupted. She knew Julia had been about to tell her the details of the meeting with Maggie's mother. And Maggie wanted to hear them . . . but not yet. Somehow she didn't feel ready.

"I told you I'd bring the boy down, and I did," Maggie continued proudly. "Those e-mails he sent you—you know the ones about that 'Kiss Me' song, and about being soul mates, and—"

"Yeah, I know the one," Julia answered, with a sheepish glance at Scoz.

"Well, it turned out that our guy Tyler had been sending the same e-mails to a bunch of girls, including that Elena chick. And he didn't even write them in the first place. Amanda wrote them."

"Amanda?" Julia repeated. "Amanda Reese?"

"Long red hair," Maggie said.

Julia nodded. "I hardly know her. She's the daughter of one of the surgeons at my dad's hospital."

"You know her a lot better now. She helped with the Tyler revenge scheme," Maggie said. "Oh, and by the way. I don't think you and Sydney Jane are speaking because I kind of screamed at her for the way she gets off on telling you ugly gossip."

"That's great. I should have done that years ago!" Julia cried. "Now back up and tell me what you did to Tyler."

"Amanda and I plastered copies of his e-mails—and the original ones from Amanda to him—all over the ladies' room. You should have seen the crowd in there.

Oh, and Tyler got slapped—twice. Once by Elena," Maggie bragged.

Julia laughed. "You're amazing," she told Maggie.

"If you want vengeance, nobody's better than Maggie," Scoz said. He gave Maggie one of his long, considering looks. "So you made it through this fiasco unscathed?"

He knows me too well, Maggie thought. "Basically," she answered, not meeting his eyes. She would keep the part about Prince Charming stomping over her glass heart to herself.

"I guess we should change outfits," Julia said, sounding reluctant.

"I can't believe you dressed me in that," Maggie said.

"She looks amazing," Scoz said. "Although it was also a clue in figuring out she was not you."

"Come on, we can change in the limo. It's parked across the street." Maggie led the way over and asked the driver to wait outside for a minute, then she and Julia climbed in back.

"There's something I've got to tell you," Julia said as she wriggled out of Maggie's black dress.

Here it comes, Maggie thought, trying to brace herself.

"Your mother, she sent you a birthday card almost every year. And she wrote you a couple of letters. They didn't say much, but they gave her phone number and made it clear that if you needed her for anything at all, she wanted you to call her."

Maggie busied herself carefully removing her wig. *I don't care,* she told herself again and again. But she couldn't stop her fingers from shaking. "She still left me," Maggie told Julia. Then she slid the Vera Wang gown over her head.

"I know," Julia said softly. "But she was just our age when she had you. Can you even imagine that? Having a baby right now—"

"If I did, I wouldn't leave it," Maggie said, her anxiety transforming itself into fury.

"I'm sure you wouldn't," Julia said mildly.

"You didn't tell her it was okay, did you?" Maggie demanded. "You didn't try to make her feel decent about herself."

Julia shook her head. "I told her I—you—were okay. And that's about it."

They didn't speak again until they were each back in their own clothes and Julia's hair was neatly tucked under the wig with the tiara still in place around the bun.

"I'm going to see you again, right?" Julia asked, a slight tremor in her voice.

"Of course," Maggie answered. "You and Scoz are going to get sick of me always being around when you want to make out."

Julia laughed. "What you did to Tyler—that was the most amazing birthday present anyone ever gave me," she said.

"I enjoyed it myself," Maggie admitted. "And you dealing with the mother thing—that was huge."

Julia seemed to want to say something, but instead she just gave Maggie a hard, quick hug. "See you soon," she mumbled. "I'll have the car take you home."

Maggie rested her head on the back of the leather seat, trying to forget that this was the same place she and Tyler had been wrapped around each other only a few hours ago.

She heard a door swing open, but it wasn't the driver getting behind the wheel. It was Scoz. "I thought Julia would have you go into the party," Maggie said. "Is she too worried her parents will flip?"

Scoz shook his head. "No, I am going in. I just wanted to give this to you." He pushed a gift bag into her hands. "When I told your dad that *you* and I were leaving the party for a while, your mother asked me to give you this. I think she was afraid you might not be coming back."

"I'm not," Maggie said. "I'm going home. The party has to be almost over by now, anyway."

"Do you want me to go with you?" Scoz asked. "Julia will understand."

Maggie felt like screaming at him not to be so nice to her. Because if he said one more nice thing, she might totally lose it and start crying. And she didn't want to do that. She was scared if she lost control, she might not get it back.

"Get out of here," Maggie said, giving Scoz a playful push. "I'll see you tomorrow."

"You sure?" he asked.

Maggie nodded, willing him away.

A moment later he was gone and the driver was back. She gave him her home address, then closed her eyes. When she opened them, she wanted to be in front of her house with this whole amazing, horrible, wonderful night behind her.

But her eyes wouldn't stay shut. They kept opening and taking little peeks at the gift bag. Finally Maggie gave up and yanked the bag open. An envelope was lying on top of a photo album.

Impatiently she ripped open the envelope. She wanted

to scan the note fast so she could rip it up and get on with her life. She unfolded the sheet of paper so quickly that one of the corners tore. Then she began to read.

Dear Maggie,

I'm writing you this note in one of the stalls in the church bathroom. I wanted to explain about the photo album in person, but I'm not sure that you'll ~~have~~ ~~have a chance to talk to me again~~ have a chance to talk to me again during the party. Thank you for giving me the time that you did.

Okay, so when you look in the photo album, you'll notice something strange. There are no pictures inside, even though there are labels for pictures. It probably seems incredibly silly, but I just pretended I had pictures. More than that, I pretended I had a life with you. I wish I had a real photo album to give to you, chock-full of real memories of you growing up. But ~~I hope you'll understand why I've~~ I hope you'll understand why I've given you this.

Love, Mom (Annette)

Maggie didn't rip up the letter. Somehow she couldn't. She dropped it back into the gift bag instead. Then she pulled out the photo album and slowly opened the cover. Her breath drew in sharply as she looked at the first page.

Me in an old rocking chair,
rocking my beautiful baby girl to sleep.

Maggie stared at the empty square until the lines around it started to blur, then she flipped the page.

Me and Maggie, covered in oatmeal.
Both laughing. My girl has quite an arm.

Maggie skipped ahead a few pages.

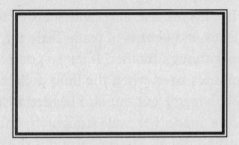

Maggie doing the wrong step at her
dance recital and looking adorable.

Maggie gently closed the photo album. She couldn't take any more. All those empty squares.

She'd always felt an empty space inside her when she thought about her mother. For the first time she realized maybe her mother had an empty space, too.

"But she left me," Maggie muttered. "It was her choice."

She closed her eyes again, trying to make the inside of her head as dark and blank as the inside of her eyelids.

It didn't work.

She opened her eyes, leaned forward, and tapped on the glass. When the divider between her and the driver rolled down, she told him she'd changed her mind about where she wanted to go. "Take me to 422 Seventh Avenue," she instructed.

Maggie lay across the seat and let the tears come. Rivers and lakes and oceans of tears. Tears for each of her sixteen years without a mother. It felt so good to let it out.

Thirty minutes later, when the limo pulled up in front of the church, Maggie got out and headed inside without hesitation. She made her way straight to the basement stairs and rushed down. She was afraid if she gave herself a second to think, she might chicken out.

It didn't take long to identify the woman who was her mother. The resemblance between them was that strong. Maggie strode over to her. "I opened the present," she blurted out.

The woman—her mother—looked surprised. "I'm . . . I'm glad," she answered.

"Look, there's this twenty-four-hour coffee shop on the corner," Maggie continued. "I thought maybe we could cut out and go there. Just to . . . whatever."

"That would be great," Maggie's mother answered, looking at Maggie with eyes exactly the color of Maggie's own.

"Okay, so, let's go," Maggie said.

Dear Me,

I don't think I would ever forget this birthday even if I didn't write myself a single word. But for those grandkids I might have someday, I figure I should say something.

Tonight, for the first time ever, I talked to my mother. I'd had a very strange day, and I ended up telling her all about it. I didn't plan to, but it just came pouring out, and she kept listening, so I kept spewing. I actually told her that I'd traded places with a stranger who looked exactly like me so I wouldn't have to meet her (my mother). And I think she actually got it, that she actually got how much it hurt me that she was able to leave me. That it hurt so much that I'd have done pretty much anything to get out of having to see her face.

She didn't give me any bull about why she did it. Maybe someday I'll want to know. But right now, I couldn't stand to hear it. Right now, anything she could say would seem completely pathetic and lame. I think maybe she got that, too.

We spent most of the time eating bad ice cream sundaes in the coffee shop and talking about guys. Well, talking about a guy. Tyler. Old me, I hope that when you read that name, it makes you laugh. Because right now, it sort of makes me feel like crying.

I totally got into the idea of this perfect, rich guy falling for me. Even though I was pretending to be someone else, it was still happening to me, you know? No guy had ever made me feel the way Tyler did. No one had ever made me feel that (gag) special. Annette (we agreed I'd call her that instead of Mom, which felt just too weird and wrong) said that one of the things she's learned is that you have to get that good feeling about yourself from yourself. Which sort of makes sense. But sort of stinks, too.

Hopefully when I write my next birthday letter to myself, I'll have found a guy who looks at me the way Scoz looks at Julia.

And as for me and Annette—well, she wants me to come out and visit. It could be cool to see California. I really don't think we'll ever get a real mother-daughter thing going. It feels too late for that. But maybe, maybe we can eventually become friends.

I just took a break and reread my letter from last year. I predicted that my Sweet Sixteen would be my best birthday ever. Was I right?

Right now, everything feels too confused for me to say for sure. So I guess I leave the call up to old me. (Hi, old me!)

Love and kisses,

Maggie

Julia and Scoz stepped into the Pierre hotel. "I should probably explain about my parents," Julia said as they crossed the lobby, their footsteps echoing on the marble floor.

Scoz hit the elevator button. "Explain away."

"They—both of them, but especially my mother—have a lot of rules. About everything. How to answer the phone. How to drink a glass of water. *Everything*."

The elevator door opened, and they stepped in. Scoz kept the door from closing with his foot. "I'm guessing they probably have a rule about dog collars only being worn on dogs," he said, fingering the leather collar around his neck.

"Definitely," Julia answered.

"I do have other clothes," Scoz told her. "I could meet your parents and your friends some other time—when I'm wearing them."

Julia grabbed his leg and jerked it all the way into the elevator. The door closed, and the elevator started up. "No, you idiot. That's not what I was trying to say. I just—" She reached out and hit the stop button. "I just don't want them to . . . to hurt your feelings."

"That's nice," Scoz said. "But I don't need you to protect me."

Julia reached for the button that would restart the elevator. Scoz caught her hand. He looked at her for a long moment, his gaze running from her Manolo Blahnik shoes to the diamond-encrusted tiara on her head. A warm shiver ran through her body, following the course of his eyes.

"It isn't a plaid skirt and a little tie, but I like this princess look," Scoz said. He pulled her up against him. "Your mother probably has a rule against kissing in elevators."

"Definitely," Julia answered. She twined her arms behind Scoz's neck. "But you know me. I was born to break the rules."

They both laughed and were still laughing when his mouth covered hers. Who knew this was what kissing could feel like? Julia thought dizzily. She'd never felt this way with Tyler. It was as if her body was melting, dissolving into Scoz's.

Scoz slowly moved his mouth away from hers and started a line of kisses down her throat, stopping at the hollow between her collarbones. "The party," he mumbled against her skin.

"The party," Julia agreed with a sigh. She gently pulled away from Scoz and restarted the elevator. When the doors opened, they walked directly into the ballroom. The effect was immediate. Group by group, people stopped talking and dancing and started staring. Well, their version of staring, which was more like a bunch of sidelong looks that were designed not to appear as anything so rude as a stare.

Julia grabbed Scoz's hand and gave it a squeeze. She led him straight up to the orchestra and borrowed the leader's microphone. "I just want to thank everyone for helping me celebrate my Sweet Sixteen," she said. "It means so much to me that all of you are here. Especially because now you'll be able to meet someone very special to me. His name is—" Julia paused as Scoz leaned close and whispered in her ear. "His name is Elliott Scozetti, Scoz for short. I hope you'll all make him feel welcome. And thank you again for being here tonight."

There was a smattering of applause as Julia handed the microphone back to the orchestra leader. "My mother is giving me the I-must-speak-with-you signal," Julia told Scoz. "Will you be okay by yourself for a little bit?"

"Sure," Scoz answered, although he looked a little uncomfortable.

Julia gave him a fast kiss on the cheek. "I'll be back as soon as I can," she promised, then walked toward her mother. She passed Amanda Reese on her way there. *Maggie said she's cool,* Julia reminded herself. "Amanda, would you mind dancing with Scoz while I talk to my mom?" she asked. "He doesn't know anyone here."

"Of course," Amanda answered. "Did you notice Tyler made an early departure? I think he was afraid if he stayed, he wouldn't make it out of here alive."

"Poor guy," Julia said sarcastically. She glanced over at her mother. Amanda followed her gaze. "I'm a little worried about making it out alive myself," Julia admitted. "Wish me luck."

"You got it," Amanda said. She gave Julia's arm an encouraging squeeze.

Julia continued toward her mother, her stomach twisting into a tighter knot with every step. "Hello," Julia said awkwardly when she reached her mom.

"Not here," Julia's mother said. She led the way to a little table as far away from the dance floor as possible and sat down. Julia took a seat across from her.

"I've seen the ladies' room," Julia's mother announced.

"So you've seen what kind of scum Tyler really is," Julia countered.

"Yes," her mother answered.

"What?" Julia exclaimed, her voice coming out much too loud.

"I don't approve of your method," Julia's mother said. "But . . . I agree that what Tyler did to you girls was wrong and that it needed to be stopped."

Julia shook her head. She didn't know what to say. This was absolutely the last thing she expected to hear her mother say. A lecture on leaving the party, yes. A lecture on bringing Scoz to the party, of course. A lecture on her treatment of Tyler, definitely. But support of any kind? No.

"It was wrong of me and your father to have pushed you so hard to continue your relationship with Tyler," her mother went on. "We arranged—with the help of Tyler's parents—for him to resume his role as escort tonight. We all thought you'd just had a minor quarrel. I didn't realize . . ." Julia's mother reached out and adjusted one of the tiny braids in Julia's bun.

Julia didn't think the braid was out of place. She thought her mother just wanted to touch her.

"I didn't realize myself," Julia admitted. "I wanted Tyler back so, so badly, even though when he broke up with me, he said I was boring and that he spent all his time with me trying to figure out how soon he could go hang out with his friends."

"He said that?" Julia's mother exclaimed, her voice filled with outrage.

"He said that," Julia confirmed. "But I still wanted him to take me back."

"How does . . . *Scoz* fit into the picture?" Julia's mother asked.

Julia glanced over her shoulder and spotted Scoz dancing with Amanda. A smile spread across her face. "I haven't known him very long," she said as she turned back to her mother. "But he's amazing. And he's . . ." She hesitated, trying to find the right words. "He's a really, really good person, Mom. I know there is no way he'd ever hurt me the way Tyler did."

"I'd like to meet this paragon," her mother told her.

"That would be great. I'll take you over there right now," Julia said.

"In a moment," Julia's mother said. "I haven't said what I wanted to say to you yet."

Now I get the lecture, Julia thought.

"I've been thinking about what you said to me out on the balcony," Julia's mother began.

Julia laced her fingers together so tightly, it hurt.

What did Maggie say to her? Why didn't Maggie tell me she said something?

"Have I really given you the impression that I care more about what people think than I do about you?" she asked, and Julia thought she heard a tiny quiver in her mother's voice.

"Of course not," Julia answered, moving automatically into good-daughter mode. Then what Scoz had called her bull meter went off big time, and Julia decided that for once she wasn't going to ignore it. "Well, at least not all the time," she qualified. "But sometimes it does seem like you care more about the outside me than the inside me."

"For example, in the way that I ignored your feelings about not wanting Tyler to attend the party after your breakup," Julia's mother said.

"Yes," Julia answered.

Her mother sighed. "I know I'm hard on you," she admitted. "I know that I'm particular about the way you dress, and your manners, and so on." She reached toward Julia's hairdo again, then pulled her hand back. "It's just that it's a hard world sometimes, Julia. For women in general, and for black women in particular. To get ahead, we can't just be equal—we have to be better. I want you to have everything you

197

want, and in my own way I've been trying to make that possible."

Julia's bull meter said that her mother was being honest with her.

"What I want is to make some of my own choices," Julia said. "Sometimes I feel like I don't have a life of my own. You've mapped out everything for me. What college I'll go to, and what sorority I'll join. What charitable organizations I'll support. And what I'll be wearing while I'm at that school and at that charity luncheon. And who will be escorting me."

Julia reached out and took her mother's hand. "I'm not you, Mom. I know you're trying to give me everything you think I want. But we don't want the same things. If I want to do charity work, which I think I do, I'd rather . . . I don't know, help build a house or something. It's not that I don't think what you do is great; it's just not what *I* want to do."

Julia stopped, breathless, and studied her mother's face, trying to gauge her reaction to what Julia had said.

The corner of her mother's mouth tilted up. "I'm remembering screaming at my mother through my bedroom door, saying almost exactly what you just said to me. 'I'm not you, Mother! I am not you!' I guess it's a part of growing up."

"Screaming? It's hard to imagine you screaming," Julia said.

"Believe it or not, I was sixteen once, too. I don't know if anyone gets through being sixteen without screaming," her mother replied. She stood up, not letting go of Julia's hand. "Come on. Take me to meet *Scoz.*"

Julia could tell how hard it was for her mother to say the name, and she appreciated the effort. "Do you see him anywhere?" she joked. Scoz was definitely easy to pick out on the dance floor, partly because he was so tall. But mostly because he was the only one in the place with purple hair and black lipstick.

The smile Scoz turned on Julia as she and her mother approached gave Julia that melting, dissolving sensation again. *He can do it without even touching me,* she realized.

"Scoz, I'd like you to meet my mother, Amelia Prescott," Julia said, fighting to be heard over the music. Amanda backed away with a little wave and a mouthed "see you later."

"Pleased to meet you, *Scoz,*" her mother said, and she shook Scoz's hand.

"You can call me Elliott if you want," he answered, getting a less strained smile out of her mother.

"You two dance," Julia ordered. "I want to find Dad and make him dance with me. I'll be right back."

She spotted her father huddled in a corner with Dr. Biehl and a couple of other doctors. On her way over to him she stopped by the orchestra and made a song request.

"I'm sorry to interrupt," Julia said as she stepped up to her father's group. "But my Sweet Sixteen wouldn't be complete without a dance with my dad."

"You're right," her father agreed, taking her hand. "We'll continue this at the staff meeting," he told the others as he and Julia headed to the dance floor. "Julia, I want you to know that I'm proud of the way you handled the Tyler situation, and I think your mother is, too, although she'd never admit it."

"Thanks," Julia said. She locked eyes on Scoz's hair and led the way over to him and her mother. "Scoz, this is my father, Donald Reed."

"I have one question for you," Julia's father said, his face serious. "How many girlfriends do you have?"

"One," Scoz answered quickly. "And that's all I want."

Julia's father nodded. There was a round of applause as the orchestra finished their number. A moment later another song started up. Scoz grinned at Julia when he recognized it—it was the same song they'd danced to in the church basement.

"Scoz and I want to teach you our go-go dance," Julia cried. She launched into a few of her moves, grooving between her mother and her father.

"Do I have to remind you that your father and I were in high school in the sixties?" Julia's mother replied. "You and your boyfriend can still learn a few things from us." And she started to jerk her arms up and down in front of her, hips twitching to the music.

"I guess there are still a *couple* of things," Julia agreed, imitating her mother's dance moves. She laughed as Scoz began imitating them, too.

Dear Me,

First of all, happy Sweet Sixteen! It was a pretty amazing birthday, wasn't it? It seems almost like a bizarre dream. Where else but in a dream would my mother be go-go dancing with a goth boy? Where else but in a dream would I be riding on a roller coaster—in Brooklyn? Where else but in a dream would I meet a girl who looks exactly like me, a girl who is probably going to be my closest friend for the rest of my life? Where else but in a dream would I fall totally, completely, madly, insanely, intensely, savagely, beautifully in love in one night?

If tonight is any indication of the year to come, all I can say is—let me keep dreaming!

I reread the letter I wrote to myself last year, and it made me laugh, and it also almost made me want to cry. All it was was a list of ways I could improve myself—like get a better grade in French and learn a vocabulary word a day. I wrote that if I followed the list carefully by today—my Sweet Sixteen—my life would be much, much better.

Well, it is much, much better. But not because I

followed the list. Because for one crazy, wonderful day I didn't follow the list. I broke all the rules. I said things I never thought I could say. And I did things I never imagined I would even want to do. And I loved it. I feel like I've been living in a cocoon my whole life and I finally broke free. And now I want more—more of everything! That's my only goal for this year, to stay the person I became tonight. If I can do that, I think on my seventeenth birthday I will be one very happy butterfly.

Love, Julia

(Actually, I decided I like that name better than JuJu after all. Guess Mom's not wrong about every-thing!)

Here's a special sneak peek of the next

Lucy,

by
Jessica Barondes

"Don't you think forty-five minutes is enough time for one person to spend in the bathroom?" my little sister Wendy pleads from the hallway.

I check the timer on the bathroom sink. "I just need ten more minutes. Wait! Actually, more like twenty. At least."

"It's my bathroom, too!" she shouts.

I watch the door rattle. Wendy has a startling amount of strength for a thirteen-year-old.

"If you have to go that bad, use Mom and Dad's," I tell her, rolling my eyes. "And while you're there, ask Dad why he went to all the trouble to design and build us a new house without enough bathrooms."

"Maybe he thought his daughters would be nice enough to *share!*" she retorts, then bangs on the door with her fist. "Ouch!"

Two days ago my family moved from Evanston, Illinois, to Skokie, another Chicago suburb about thirty minutes north. My dad, who is an architecture professor at Northwestern University, gave the new house every modern amenity. Unfortunately he forgot the simple detail that one bathroom is just not enough for two teenage girls. Especially when one of them is in the process of giving herself a secret makeover.

"Why can't you leave me alone?" I plead. "I'm busy in here, Wendy."

"I just want to know what you're doing," Wendy admits, her voice softening. "Come on, Lucy. Please."

I stare at myself in the mirror and smile. "You'll know soon enough."

"Even sooner would be better," she begs.

I giggle to myself when I imagine how Wendy would react if she saw me right now. Her jaw would probably hit the floor. My hair is sticking up, covered in black goop and shoved into a plastic bag. A green mud mask covers my face, and my left forearm is bright red from trying to scrub off any remaining traces of a henna tattoo.

Suddenly I feel a rush of desire to let Wendy in on it. To finally tell someone about the secret mission that I'm finally completing after five months of obsessing and planning. I swing open the door.

"Agggh!" Wendy screams. An even better reaction than I imagined. "What are you *doing* to yourself?"

I grab her hand and pull her inside. "Shhh!" I whisper harshly. "I don't want Mom and Dad to see me until the morning. I want to surprise them with the complete new me, and I'm not nearly finished."

I plop down on the toilet seat and begin removing my vamp toenail polish with a cotton ball. I've already scrubbed my fingernails bare.

"What new you?" Wendy asks, baffled.

I toss the blackened cotton ball and moisten another one with the remover. "Isn't it obvious?" I ask, glancing up at her. "I'm giving myself a makeover."

She wrinkles her forehead. "Why?"

"With dad moving us out of our old neighborhood and into this new house, it's just, well, an opportunity for me," I say with a shrug. "To start fresh at a new school. Clean up my act."

"You only got into a *little* trouble," Wendy says.

"I was put in detention for a month!" I cringe at the memory. An entire month of total, complete after-school boredom.

"Just for passing a note to Leah?" Wendy asks, standing next to me in front of the mirror and running a hand through her shaggy blond hair. "It was cruel and unusual punishment, if you ask me."

"What about when I was practically arrested?" I

remind her. "I had to do fifty hours of community service."

"You were an innocent bystander!" Wendy says indignantly, her eyes widening. "Even on the surveillance video it never shows you participating in the vandalism. Besides, you get straight A's. They should've cut you some slack."

I smile at her and wish other people saw me the way my little sister does. I even wish *I* admired myself as much as she does. In Wendy's eyes, I can do no wrong.

"You don't know what it's like to be in high school yet, Wendy. Once you get a bad reputation, it's just over." I toss the cotton ball into the trash can and scrape away the remaining polish stuck around my cuticles with my fingernail. "It's like the hours between the first and last bell are total misery."

I glance over at the timer. Seven minutes left. Seven minutes until I'm restored to my original hair color and can begin my attempt to reinvent myself.

"I thought you were cool as a blond," Wendy says.

"Oh, you just liked it because we looked more alike," I tell her, tousling her hair.

Wendy has always tried to follow in my footsteps. When I was into wearing high-tops with skirts in the seventh grade, it was harmless. And when it involved sewing buttons all over my backpack in the eighth, I may have been annoyed by the little copycat, but my mom and dad thought it was sweet. But when I started high school last year, everything changed. No parents would ever hope that their adorable and spunky younger child would have a role model as messed up as I was.

It had started innocently enough. A week before freshman year began, my best friend, Leah, and I decided to do some experimenting. We were just tired of who we were. We were never in the in crowd, never in the out crowd; we were just two Chicago girls with warm winter coats and maybe a slight flair for the creative—like making our own beaded jewelry and using our old jeans to make purses and hats.

I don't know if it was our teenage hormones or what (although I read in an article about the teenage brain that hormones really do make you do crazy things), but we suddenly felt daring and ready for a change.

The truth was, it did seem sort of boring to always have the same exact hairstyle. I mean, my class picture looked the same every single year! So in a moment of true courageousness I had my long brown hair chopped off and dyed platinum blond. Then I adopted a skintight wardrobe to go with my new cutting edge 'do. Leah joined me in an image change, adding a green tint to her blond hair and a pierce to her perfect ski jump nose and literally dumping her entire closet of clothes into a vat of black dye.

My mom and dad were clearly not happy, but they didn't officially freak on me until the day that Wendy had to go and do a number on herself. In an attempt to be just like me, she cut off all her hair in the bathroom. (Thankfully, no dye was necessary in her case.)

When my mom saw her, she grabbed a clump of Wendy's shorn hair from the sink, stalked into my room, and handed it to me. It was proof of what a bad influence I was.

She said she felt like she didn't even know me any-more. But the truth was, I didn't know who I was, either, really. I was just trying to figure it out. I'm *still* trying to figure it out.

"What's Leah going to think?" Wendy asks.

"I don't know," I say sheepishly, staring at my reflection.

To be honest, I've gone way out of my way to hide a lot from Leah ever since my dad announced the big move. As I began to feel like I was getting into something that wasn't quite right for me, Leah only seemed more and more interested in being in the fringe. She added a pierce to her navel and started talking about getting a tattoo.

She was bummed enough that I was leaving the neighborhood. If she knew I was going back to the old me, it would just be way too much for her to handle.

Suddenly I feel a pang of nostalgia mixed with guilt.

"I really miss her," I say thoughtfully. "Already."

In spite of all the things that have happened, Leah is my oldest and dearest friend in the world. We became inseparable when she moved to Evanston from Detroit when we were eight. The best times of my life have been spent alongside Leah, just giggling in my bedroom, walking home from school together, and going along on her family vacations to Lake Michigan every summer.

Of course I'll tell her about the changes I'm going through. Maybe not tonight during our scheduled nine o'clock call, but soon. As soon as I get a better handle on it.

"I miss her, too." Wendy sighs. "She was a lot of fun, you know."

"Well, as soon as she gets her license, I'm sure she'll be coming over here all the time. Maybe she can move into the guest room."

7

"That's already reserved for Cleo and Amanda," Wendy says, listing her two best friends from home. "She'll have to bunk with you."

I stand up and study myself in the mirror again, this time focusing in on my ears. I have four pierces on each side. The first ones were a gift that I begged my parents to give me for my tenth birthday. My mom held my hand as the manager of Forty Karats held a gun to my ear and bestowed me with two little gold studs. The second, third, and fourth came courtesy of Leah, an ice cube, a needle, and a strong thrust.

I slip out the earrings at the very top and work my way down until I'm left with only my original single pierces. "Want to borrow these?" I ask, handing the fistful of silver studs and tiny hoops Wendy's way.

She looks at me like they're contaminated. "Not if you don't want them."

I shrug and place them on the counter. There are now three ugly red puncture marks in each of my ears.

"Do you think I'm scarred for life?" I ask, inspecting each lobe closely.

"I'm sure they'll heal up eventually. So did you buy new clothes, too?" Wendy raises her eyebrows.

I grin, knowing I'm in for another Wendy freak-out. "Go look in my closet."

Wendy darts out of the bathroom, and I hear the door of my walk-in bang against the wall. "Oh my God! You really are serious about this."

I saved up my money and did my best to buy the basics of a stylishly conservative wardrobe. Maybe a little on the preppy side—there are lots of pastels, loafers, and cardigan sweaters. A big contrast to the leather jacket, combat boots, platform shoes, and row-of-black-Lycra attire that I've stored in the back of the closet.

"This stuff isn't you. Is it?" Wendy asks me.

I dab cover-up on the piercing scars. "Maybe. I never really felt right about that last look. I tried to dress cool, but I always felt a little awkward. I'm trying something new."

The timer dings.

"It just seems so sudden," Wendy gripes. "Hey, do you think I'd fit in this pink sweater?"

"Not until I've worn it," I tell her. "And it's not sudden. I started planning this whole thing when Daddy first told us about the move. I mean, c'mon, when was the last time you saw me get my hair cut?"

"True," Wendy agrees.

I slip the plastic bag off my head. "I found out about this hair tonic in a magazine that's supposed to make your hair grow faster. I think it might have worked."

"I can't believe you didn't tell me," Wendy complains.

"Since when do I tell you anything?" I ask, fiddling with the faucets to make lukewarm water.

"Well, I don't know. But since you didn't tell Leah, you would think you'd need to tell someone." Wendy returns to the bathroom and takes the spot on the toilet seat. "I could have gone shopping with you."

"Oh, lucky me," I joke.

Wendy wrinkles her face and sticks out her tongue as a retort.

I giggle. "Here goes." I dunk my head into the sink and watch the dye trickle down the drain.

"So what is this new look supposed to be?" Wendy asks, handing me a towel once I've been thoroughly rinsed. "What are you going for?"

"I don't know. I . . . I was going to try to see if I could . . ." I look down. I just can't say it.

"What?"

"It's shallow."

"So? Tell me."

I wrap the towel around my head like a turban. "Dress the way the popular clique did back at Lincoln," I say, referring to what is now my ex–high school.

Wendy smirks. "You want to be in the *in crowd?*"

"No," I say quickly. "I just want to try to be something different than I was."

"This is going to be so cool!" Wendy says, jumping up from her seat. "Will you let me hang out with all your new friends? We could go to the movies together . . . and I'm sure there'll be tons of great parties, too."

"Don't get all excited," I tell her, feeling a little lump of nervousness in my stomach. "Who knows if I'll even make any friends? This is the end of my sophomore year. Everybody probably already has their little groups. Maybe no one will even talk to me."

"Oh, come on," Wendy says, looking at my reflection in the mirror. "Who wouldn't want to be your friend? You're smart, funny, pretty. . . ."

I smile thoughtfully at Wendy as she continues listing off what she considers to be my virtues. I wish I could have that kind of confidence about myself. I do know that I'm smart, or at least that my grades are strong. But I've always felt a little awkward about the way people perceive me. When I was younger and dressed a little on the kooky side, it seemed like people thought of me as kind of an off-the-wall bookworm. And when I started dressing like a club girl, I could see the glaring, disapproving eyes of my teachers

11

and the majority of my peers. Plus I saw how quickly Leah and I were welcomed into the alternative group at school. In other words, what I've figured out first-hand is that people make huge assumptions about you based on the way you look. Which is why I've decided to try to dress like a member of the mainstream. To see if that isn't the place where I can finally feel comfortable about who I am.

". . . and you have a *perfect* body. Plus you don't even get zits any more."

"Wendy," I say with a laugh. "Can you write that all down for me so I can look at it when I'm freaking out tomorrow?" I pull the towel off my head and attempt to get a comb through the knots in my hair.

"I have a good feeling about it, Lucy. I think you're going to do amazing." She pulls her hair off her face and looks at herself in the mirror. "Now, what about me? I have to start at a new school, too. Can you help me figure out what I should wear?"

I glance at her reflection. "Of course."

About the Author

Melinda Metz is the author of the ongoing young adult book series *Roswell High,* which is the basis of the WB television series *Roswell.* Melinda has also written books for several book series, including *The New Adventures of Mary-Kate and Ashley, Ghosts of Fear Street,* and *Goosebumps Presents.* She lives in Manhattan with a pen-eating dog named Dodger.

Enter the

M2M *Sweet 16*

sweepstakes today

(See following pages for details)

Hello and greetings to our new fans and friends.

The two of us met when we were both five years old in a small town just outside of Oslo, Norway, and it wasn't long before we started singing and dancing together. To make a long story short, one of our demos ended up at Atlantic Records and we got a worldwide deal! What you'll hear is the result of a year of really hard work (and lots of fun!!!).

Hope you enjoy it!!